CW01497043

WARNING:

This book contains handcuffs, hair pulling, perverted Valentine's cards, and all other sorts of naughty. This book is NOT intended for anyone who dislikes hot sex scenes, bad boys, or nerds with kinky sides. Read at your own risk.

Books by C.M. Stunich

C.M. STUNICH

SARIAN ROYAL

to those of you who were brave enough to pick up a book with handcuffs on the front cover. I heart the fuck out of you.

CHAP 1
GOOD COP, BAD COP
ONE WEEK UNTIL UNDERAPPRECIATED SINGLES' DAY

"I'm not going to touch your dick just because you gave me a box of chocolates." I handed the heart shaped box back to Quinn and tried to step around him. When he put out his arm to stop me, I rolled my eyes and crossed my arms over my chest. "It's not even Valentine's Day yet," I told him, totally confused as to why a guy who'd never even spoken to me before was now suddenly interested in providing me with presents.

"No dick touching necessary," he told me as he

handed the chocolates back and smiled. "In fact," he continued as he stepped forward and brushed a bit of my hair away from my face. "You don't have to do any touching at all." He paused, grinning wickedly, like a porn star or an underwear model or something. It was dirty, practiced, and totally fucking sexy. "Unless you want to." And then Quinn turned and disappeared down the hallway giving me a long, uninterrupted view of his ass.

Wow.

The campus Casanova was hitting on me.

The question now, of course, was why. Why, after all this time, was he suddenly interested? Was it because Valentine's Day was right around the corner and he didn't have a date? Nah. I shook my head and clutched the box of chocolates to my chest. Guys like Quinn didn't give a shit about Valentine's Day. Besides, there were a hundred girls that would throw themselves at his feet if he even bothered to toss a glance their way.

With a sigh, I continued down the hallway, convinced that men were a different species altogether, one that I would never understand. I was so busy thinking about

Fuck Valentine's Day

Quinn and his sharp, blue eyes that I ended up running into a big, broad, *delicious* chest. The candy flew out of my hands, suspended in the air like a cluster of chocolate rain drops and fell to the floor at my feet.

"Sorry," I mumbled as I knelt down and started to scoop them up. I didn't want to admit it, but I was kind of sad about my Quinn candy. It was my only real hope of ever nibbling on anything that came from a boy like him … Quinn Prentis. Sigh. *Waaaaay out of my league, box of chocolate or no.*

"No, it was my fault," said a soft-spoken voice from above me. I glanced up, and up, and up. It was Preston Ellis, the nerdy guy from my calculus class. He was dressed in a hunter green sweater over a white button up with a burgundy tie underneath. He had pretty eyes, but they were hidden behind a pair of thick, black glasses. His face was strong, masculine, all hard lines and edges. *Drool worthy.* "Please, accept my apologies," he whispered as he knelt down and used his notebook to shovel the rest of the chocolates into the box top. "I'll have to give you some later." He looked over the top of his glasses at me, brown eyes crinkling slightly around the edges as he smiled. I was assuming he meant chocolates, but if he wanted to give me something else later ... I shook my head to clear it.

"No, um, that's alright, but thanks." *I am way too horny for a virgin. Or maybe because I am a virgin? God, I need to get laid.* We stood up in unison and paused awkwardly next to one another.

"Sorry," he said again as a group of giggling girls burst into the hallway and split around us like a wave. "See you around." Preston ducked away to my left, head down, books tucked under his arm and suddenly, I felt this sharp pinch on my ass. I spun around, but there were so many blonde haired, blue-eyed volleyball players that I was having a hard time seeing who might have done it.

Oddly enough, it never struck me that it might've been Preston Ellis.

I trudged to my calc class, rubbing my ass and

Fuck Valentine's Day

contemplating all the reasons that Quinn Prentis might have decided to give *me* a box of chocolates. We had a ton of classes together, but that didn't mean he knew me. Hell, I didn't even think he knew *of* me. I was sort of forgettable sometimes. I had legs for days sure (modesty – not one of my traits), but my hair was long and brown and boring. My eyes were moderately sized and my lips were flat.

"Maybe he thinks I'm an easy lay?" I said and unfortunately, the words were not confined to the depths of my thick skull. That's right, I said them *out loud.* I flushed a nice shade of pink, something that would look real nice on a Valentine's Day card, and slipped into the nearest seat before anyone could look up and see what idiot was blathering their ridiculous thoughts for all the world to hear.

I glanced around surreptitiously, trying to catch sight of either Quinn or Preston. A little eye candy never hurt anyone after all. Besides, if Quinn really was interested in me, wouldn't he be looking for me, too? Then I found him and realized how stupid I was being. My rational mind jumped in there with a nice, little quip. *This is why we turned him down, Princess.* I told her to fuck off as I watched Quinn hit on a pair of coeds in the back row.

"Jackass," I mumbled and nearly exploded out of my skin when a warm hand brushed against my arm. I glanced up and found Preston standing above me with a stack of papers in his left hand. He was staring down at me with this little smirk on his face that seemed at odds with the sweater and the dorky glasses.

"It's kind of big," he told me as his fingers flitted across my arm and gave me goose bumps. "Do you think you can handle it?" I stared at the hottest geek the world had ever seen and tried not to gawp. And failed. *You are practically drooling, Andi, shut your damn mouth.* It wasn't until a bit of saliva hit me in the tits that I managed to get a hold of myself.

"Huh?" I asked, convinced that I was dreaming and that I was only seconds away from seeing Preston whip out his cock and show me the meaning of the word *sore.* I mean, the man had massively huge hands with long, sexy fingers and his feet were at least twice the size of mine. I wasn't claiming to be an expert on men or anything (virgin, remember?), but I did watch a lot of porn and there is definitely a correlation between hands, feet, and cocks.

"The stack," he said as he handed me a sheet of formulas. "It's really heavy. Can you handle it?"

"Oh." I took the papers from him and tried not to sound disappointed. *Damn it. I could've used a nice wet daydream to start the day off right.* "Of course." Preston winked at me and ran one his big hands down his flat, sexy chest which looked damn good, even in that ugly sweater, and turned away with a wink. Seconds later, the papers (who were absolutely, one hundred percent out to get me), slid from my hands and flitted across the floor in all directions like a flock of birds.

Preston paused and glanced back at me, dark brows raised skeptically.

Way to impress, Andi. Nice job.

I'd been stalking Preston Ellis for the past two years, signing up for the classes I knew he'd be in, watching his ass as he wrote up formulas as our class's student assistant, and I'd failed to impress him. Heck, I'd failed to impress any guy ever. I was sort of an epic fail when it came to dudes. Twenty-two, perpetually single, unbelievably horny. *That's me!*

"Let me get those," he said as I climbed out of my seat and bent down. Hilarity ensued and we ended up butting heads *hard.* Let's just say Preston Ellis left that class with a bleeding forehead, and I left with the world's bluest balls. Or ovaries? How does that work? Aw, fuck it. You know what I meant.

Case in point: I was horny as hell and there was nobody, and I mean *nobody,* that was going to be able to do a damn thing about it.

I headed to the store after class, drawn by a sale on Valentine's Day candy and wine. Last year, I'd spent the stupid holiday alone. This year probably wouldn't be any different. I mean, it's not like I was desperate for a man or anything, it's just … it would be nice to have a date on Valentine's Day for a change.

You didn't have to be so rude to Quinn, I told myself

Fuck Valentine's Day

as I navigated between necking couples whose osculating I could only handle so much of. *He was just giving you chocolates. I mean, even if all he really wanted was sex, why not give it to him?*

I tripped over the shoes of a man emerging from the *Personal Hygiene* aisle and fell face first into a bin of Valentine's Day pins. I almost screamed as I was submerged in white buttons with red and pink hearts, but before I could drown on Cupid kitsch, a strong hand was being wrapped around my waist. The mystery man pulled me out and spun me around.

It was Quinn. Again.

"Hey there, beautiful," he said as he kept his arm wrapped around my waist. "If I didn't know any better, I'd say you were stalking me." I raised my eyebrows at him and then my eyes caught on his opposite hand, and what was clutched in it. A box of condoms.

"Getting ready for the big day already?" I asked him as I tried to untangle myself. All the while, the skin on my lower back between my shirt and jeans was tingling from the touch of Quinn's fingers. He stepped back and raised his hands in surrender.

"You got me," he said with a wink. "After all, I knew you'd agree to come out with me eventually. Pick you up tomorrow maybe?"

"Right," I said as I tried to walk away. Quinn stopped me with a hand on my arm, drawing my eyes around to his. They were so bright in his tan face, like two portals to the Caribbean. I could so vacation in there.

"You sure you don't want to hang out with me tomorrow? I'd make it worth your while." I paused and gave Quinn a once over that started at his red Mohawk and traveled all the way down to his bulging biceps, tight T-shirt, and landed on the bump in the front of his jeans. I wanted to say yes, but I was also ornery and had a bit of an acidic tongue that my mother could never quite curb. I think I was also allergic to being nice.

"What's my name?" I asked finally, convinced that if he could at least get this, I'd go. I so wanted to. Quinn was … Quin was wow. Every girl on campus (and several boys) knew his name and they all wanted to fuck him. If they said otherwise, they were lying. He bit his lip and nibbled it for several moments before snapping his fingers.

Fuck Valentine's Day

"I don't know your name per se, but I know you're the super hot chick that usually sits in the front row of our lit class." Quinn threw me his sexiest grin from a mouth full of super white teeth. It made the lines of tattoos on his neck shift, drawing my attention to the color that crawled up the sides of his throat in artful swirls. It was a good trick, but not good enough.

"Sorry, Quinn," I said and then turned on my heel and tried to hide behind the row of pink chocolates. He followed me and stood close by, pretending to be interested in a gold box with a red bow on the top. I moved around the other side of the shelf, into an aisle full of stuffed animals. I only lasted thirty seconds there because the purple bears with kissy-faces scared the shit out of me. I went back to the candy aisle. Quinn was still there. "Stop following me," I hissed at him as I picked up an abandoned hand basket and started tossing candy into it. Quinn turned to face me, the chains hanging from his belt jingling as he moved.

"Sorry," he said as he turned away. "Just buying a present for a beautiful girl." And then he disappeared around the corner. I sat down on the floor and put my hands over my face, dragging them down slowly as I tried to wipe away some of my stress. *This is why you're still a virgin,* I told myself as I looked up and came face to face with a display of half priced Hershey's Kisses. I grabbed three bags.

A few seconds later, Quinn came back around the corner with the chocolates, a receipt, and a condom tucked under the bow on top of the candy.

"This is for you," he said as he sat the present down on the floor next to me. As he stood up and moved around the corner, tight, sexy body disappearing from view, I called out to him.

"Andrea Fisher," I said, and he paused, laying one hand on the white metal shelving next to him. "Andi for short."

"Thanks, beautiful," he said and then he was gone.

CHAP 2
WHAT THE HELL IS THIS?
SIX DAYS UNTIL "YEAH, I'M MARRIED, SO SUCK IT!" DAY

I woke up an hour late and blew a big test in biology because I spent all night masturbating to Quinn Prentis and wearing fuzzy, plastic handcuffs that I bought at the store. I kind of felt stupid handcuffing one of my wrists to the headboard, but I did it anyway and had the best orgasm *ever.*

"Thank you, sir," I said as I unhooked myself and shook out my sore arm. I threw on a pair of white and blue striped pajamas and waddled down to the kitchen, just a tad sore down there from my new dildo. It was called the *Randy,* and it was my special friend on nights when I didn't have a warm body next to mine (that's every night).

My friend/roommate, Genevieve Pares, was busy necking with her fuck buddy, Lance, on my couch. They kind of did other things on my couch, so I was always covering it with towels and such to catch *juices,* and inevitably all my other friends would ask, "Why the fuck do you have seven towels covering up your couch?" I never quite knew how to answer that question.

"Hey guys," I said. They ignored me which was okay because they sort of did this often. I kind of liked to think of them as people I could confide in. You know, the really good couple you could tell everything to because they're both your friends? Well, except for the fact that they never heard what I had to say. Oh, and they weren't a couple. That's okay, I made do. I just told new acquaintances that my boyfriend's name was Randy and my best friends were Genevieve and Lance and nobody asked otherwise. "I was thinking of going on a date with this guy, Quinn Prentis, because he's like … " I pulled a

Fuck Valentine's Day

gallon of milk from the fridge and dropped it when Genevieve moaned like a wild animal. White liquid shot out everywhere, making me even more depressed for the upcoming holiday. *That's the only white liquid that I'm going to see spraying across my kitchen.*

"Lance! Lance! Lance!"

"Anyway," I continued as I grabbed a rag and started wiping up the floor. "Quinn is seriously the hottest guy I've ever seen, and I didn't think I had a chance with him, but ... "

"Genevieve, ride me, baby!"

"Oh yeah, you know it!"

"He actually seems interested in me." I threw the rag in the sink and picked up the empty milk jug, tossing it into the garbage can next to the counter as the couch springs started to creak. "I just don't know ... I kind of wanted to keep my V for someone special." I sighed and traded my cereal bowl for a plate. Guess it was toaster pastry time again.

I threw a couple of the fatty, flaky rectangles in and held up a hand to shield my eyes from my roommate as I made my way to the front door and checked the mail. I

21

was expecting a Valentine's card from my mom (shut up, okay, I know that's fucking lame) with some money it and hadn't gotten the chance to look yesterday. Lo and behold, there were two pink envelopes in the mail that day.

"Hot damn," I said as I carried them both inside past the fuck buddies and sat down at the breakfast bar. One of the envelopes had a stamp on one corner and my mom's return address on the other. The second envelope was blank except for my name.

Andrea Annette Fisher.

"Huh," I said as I slid my thumb under the pink paper and opened the envelope. The first thing that came out was a Valentine's Day card with a sexy man on the front. He had abs like the Grand Canyon, all mountains and valleys, and a *huge* bulge in his red and white underwear. *Yummy.*

Bitch, please! You thought Cupid was a freaking baby? Check out this bow and arrow.

I laughed as I reached over the counter and grabbed at my toaster pastries. Something slipped from inside the card and fell to the floor, picture side down. I set my plate down in front of me and looked at the message inside. It was blank except for an address written in neat, tiny letters, all caps. I didn't recognize the place, so I set it aside and climbed off the stool.

"Fuck me hard, Lance! Now! Oh yeah, right there!"

"What the hell is this … " My voice trailed off as I grabbed the picture and flipped it over. "Holy cock!" I yelped as I came face to face with said object. There was a penis on the picture, a real, live penis with wrinkles and everything. It was as big as my *Randy,* long and wide, circumcised *perfection.* "Genevieve, seriously, come here and look at this."

I turned the picture around and around trying to find some sort of identifying information. There was none. Except for the address in the card. I sat back on the stool and examined the photo for realism. *Was this thing Photoshopped?* There was a man's hand wrapped around the base of the cock and little droplets of moisture from a shower or lube or something. I, myself, was getting wet just looking at the damn thing. That was even *before* I noticed the little silver ring through the skin near the head of Mystery Man's cock. It was a Prince Albert.

"I'm coming," Genevieve started shouting behind me, and I took that as my cue to grab my quickie breakfast, my cards, and my penis pic and get the hell out of there.

I found Quinn Prentis hitting on some girls near the door to our lit class.

The act infuriated me to no end. *Told you to avoid this prick,* my rational mind said as she stuck her tongue out at me. I had the picture clutched in my hand and marched right up to the biggest bad boy on campus.

"Think you're such a stud?" I said, and the two girls he was flirting with moved away like I was poisoned. I mean, come on, I wasn't that scary was I? Five foot nine, thin as a rail, brown hair, brown eyes, I was just your average girl. Maybe they saw something in my face that day that told them to back the fuck off, maybe it was instinctual, some old forgotten woman vs. woman thing? I have no fucking clue.

Fuck Valentine's Day

Quinn held up his hands and sucked in his lower lip, big, blue eyes all wide and innocent. I almost swooned, but I held my ground.

"Hey there, beautiful."

"It's Andi," I said, acidic tongue wagging at full force. "So, you just leading me on or what? Why ask me out? Give me chocolates?"

"I'm just hanging out. You know I was waiting for you, right? Didn't see you in bio, so I thought something was wrong."

"Uh huh," I said, about to thrust the picture in his face and demand that he explain himself. Then he stepped forward and his should-be-illegal-because-it's-so-tight T-shirt rode up his belly and flashed me wet worthy abs and a trickle of dark hair along with some brightly colored tattoos. Tattoos that were most certainly *not* in my penis picture.

"I'm all yours for tonight if you come clubbing with me. I won't even look at another woman. Pinky promise?" he asked, and I stood there like a deer in the headlights. *If Quinn didn't send the pic, who did?* I had just sort of assumed it was him. I mean, who else would've done it? Besides, it was pierced. Don't all bad boys have pierced junk?

"Um," I began as he moved closer to me and sent the hairs on my arms standing to attention. He moved like a panther, all sleek and muscular and *deadly.* I almost drooled. *Maybe he took it before he was tatted?*

"What have you got in your hand, beautiful?" he asked, apparently allergic to using my first name. I took a step back and flicked my eyes back and forth. Did I have a stalker? Was he watching me carry his picture even now? Masturbating to it? And why was that idea making me so wet between the thighs?

"Is your dick pierced?" I blurted, and Quinn paused. Then he stood there and stared at me with a blank facial expression that made me sick to my stomach. I kept myself from bolting by attaching my eyes to his belly button. Now that, *that* was pierced. My Mystery Man's wasn't. Shit.

"Um, no," Quinn said, and that was that. "Save you a seat?" I turned around and ran all the way to the parking lot.

Fuck Valentine's Day

I plugged the address into my phone and drove my old, beat-up Geo Metro through town like a crazy person. When I arrived at my destination, I found out that it was actually a gym, and not just any regular, old gym. It was a *boxing* gym. It was big and old and crumbly and *tough* looking. I sat there for the longest time glancing between the picture and the gym, watching men come out in droves, women, too. They were all tough, ripped, and sexy, plus they were soaked in sweat. How was I supposed to know who my stalker was?

I swallowed my anxiety and stuffed the picture into my purse, keeping only the card clutched in my hand. I got a lot of stares (probably because I was wearing a pink sweater instead of a black sports bra) as I made my way inside and came face to chest with a massive, hulking man with a permanent scowl and – get this – a scar down the right side of his face. How cliché is that?

"Can I help you?" he asked as I tried to peer around

him at the various punching bags, rings, and exercise equipment. I don't know what I was looking for. I mean, it's not as if my Mystery Man's Prince Albert was going to be displayed for all the world to see. I'm not sure what I was expecting to see or do there, but I had to ask. I mean, you would, too, right?

"Yeah, um, I'm looking for someone." I held out the Valentine's Day card and the big man looked down at it with a grunt. When he crossed his arms over his chest, I seriously thought his muscles were going to explode through the skin on his arms. They were as big around as my thighs!

"Name?"

"Well, I don't exactly know that … " I said as I dropped my hand to my side and tried not to crinkle my card. It was my only clue. Why I cared, and why I was seeking this guy out and *not* filing criminal stalking/indecent exposure charges against him was kind of beyond me. Something about it was intriguing in a kind of weird, fucked up way. Guess I was just the world's kinkiest virgin.

"What's he look like? He the guy from the card?" I

snorted and the big man shifted, giving me a whiff of jockstrap and old socks. *Eww.* I tucked some errant strands of hair behind my ear and tried to remain calm. So what if a good dozen men and a handful of women were checking out my ass from the free weight section of the gym? *I'm wearing my good jeans, so the view should check out okay.*

"No, um, he's not this guy." I lifted up the card and examined Cupid. *Damn.* "I mean, I don't think so. I guess, I wish he was this guy, you know?" I laughed, and it echoed strangely off the cement floors and brick walls. Nobody else joined in. I took a deep breath and focused on my task. "See, I don't *exactly* know what this man looks like. I … " Scar Face's nostrils flared, and I took an involuntary step back. What was I supposed to say? That my guy had his junk pierced and abs like rocks? *They've been in the locker room, so maybe if you ...* Stopped that train of thought before I started going on about this seven inch cock in my picture and how I really, really wanted to meet it. "Okay, so I think I'll just go and come back later." The man snorted through his nose like a bull, and I turned on my heel and booked it out of there.

When I got to my car, there was a note taped to the driver's side window.

Glad you came to find me. Want another clue? Call Me. This was followed, of course, by a phone number. There was a conversation that played out in my head that went something like this:

Rational Andi: *Are you fucking serious? Call the cops and turn this bitch in BEFORE he cuts off your head and hangs it in his living room as a light fixture.*

Horny Andi: *This is just a silly prank, Rational Andi. Don't be such a cock blocker! Let's have some fun for once. If it wasn't for you, I'd have gotten laid by Jake Tandor senior year.*

Rational Andi: *Jake was a douche! You're so lucky I protected your cherry berry from that prick.*

Horny Andi: *I don't have a cherry. I masturbate with an eight inch rubber cock.*

Rational Andi: *I meant your metaphysical cherry, Gawd.*

Horny Andi: *I'm shutting you out. I think we have an unhealthy relationship.*

Rational Andi: *Go fuck yourself.*

Fuck Valentine's Day

And then I dialed the number. The phone rang for awhile and then went to voice mail. Disappointed and in no way willing to leave a message, I hung up, vowing to try again later. Seconds after, a text arrived.

Check under your favorite chair in calculus tomorrow. Signed, Your Secret Admirer

I stared at it for a long while, thoroughly convinced that *secret admirer* was way less creepy than *stalker.*

Rational Andi: *Lampshade.*

I ignored her and went about my day with the dick pic in my back pocket.

CHAP 3
GIRL MEETS STALKER...
I mean BOY
FIVE DAYS UNTIL YOU CRY YOURSELF TO SLEEP WATCHING MEG RYAN AND TOM HANKS DAY

I woke to a very loud, very raucous knock at my door. I rolled over and groaned, assuming that Gen and her boy toy were busy fucking against it. Wouldn't have been the first time.

"Andi, there's some *super* hot guy here to see you." And then she gave me a very gracious five seconds to react to the news, roll over and squint at the door as it opened and in walked Quinn. He was wearing a black tank that showed off his beefy shoulders and various skull tattoos. He had plugs in his lower earlobes today and a beanie on his head, covering up his Mohawk do. Little bits of red hair stuck out the front like bangs.

"Sorry," he said as he made a sort of grimacing face at my current state, all sleepy eyed and disoriented. "But your friend said you were in desperate need of something and that I should come up here?" I tried to glare at Genevieve, but she was already gone, probably scouting out her next boy. Or girl. Gen swung both ways.

"Um," I struggled to sit up and felt a strange pull in my shoulder. Pain rocketed through my body making me scream out in pain. It felt like Scar Face was behind me, twisting my arm into a very awkward, very uncomfortable position.

"Shit!" Quinn said as he leapt to my rescue and … unhooked … my … handcuffs. He held the furry purple plastic cuffs in one hand and stared at me with his baby blues. I was sitting with my teeth clenched, arm lying across my knees as I tried to breathe through my nose. *I fell asleep with them on again. Masturbating to … the dick pic. Wow, this is awkward.*

"There's a rational explanation to all of this," I

explained as Quinn stared at me and a rictus grin spread across his smooth face. He might've been the 'bad boy' archetype, but he didn't have quite as nice a face as Preston, not as manly. Quinn had a rounder jaw and smoother cheeks whereas Preston had a nice, strong jaw and bones sculpted by the Gods. *And you're comparing them why? Why are you even thinking about Preston Ellis?*

"You like to get your kink on, right?" Quinn said and then he kissed me. Just leaned over the bed and kissed me. He started off with a bang, too. There was none of that sweet, romance-y stuff where we like, *tasted each other's souls* or anything. He just shoved his hot, slick tongue in my mouth and started Frenching the shit out of me.

Rational Andi: *Kick this bitch's ass! Who the hell does he think he is?*

Horny Andi: *I am feeding you cyanide first chance I get. Shut your damn mouth. This guy is* HOT.

I reached up and wrapped my arms around Quinn's neck, pulling him down between my knees where I could feel his hot, hard body very clearly against mine. He had an erection that was poking me through the thin blanket that separated us. Did I mention I wasn't wearing any panties? Kind of took 'em off to masturbate. I had brief thoughts of remorse that Quinn *wasn't* my Mystery Man and vice versa, but decided to roll with it for a second. I mean, Quinn Prentis was kissing *me*. Seriously, how cool was that? Granted, I had turned him down before, but that was only because Rational Andi was in control. Now that that bitch was poisoned, I could finally get a nibble of this boy with the hard ass and the sexy growl that he was not afraid to use as he reached down and unbuttoned his pants.

Rational Andi: *I'm not dead, yet, bitch. Get a grip on yourself, seriously.*

I struggled to say something to Quinn, anything at all. No words would come out, just moans as he freed his cock from his pants and proceeded to rub it against my clit through the blanket. *Is this dry humping?* I wondered and then, *No, this is at least wet humping. Oh my god ... Wet humping ... Yes!*

"You are so hot, beautiful," Quinn said as he pressed his mouth to mine and knocked our teeth together. It was kind of hot. "Hottest calc babe I know."

"I'm not exactly a babe," I said and then, "Oh!" as Quinn started nibbling my ear. I reached my hands under his shirt and felt along his muscles. They were rock solid and slick with just a bit of sweat (probably because Gen left the heater on *all* the damn time). I explored his shoulders and upper back, dragged my nails along his flesh, and opened my legs. Quinn didn't move the blanket though, just kept his rhythm going until we were both moaning like alley cats.

Bang! Zip! BAM!

"Holy shit!" I screamed as I came, wrapping my legs around Quinn's ripped midsection, squeezing his body in a vice grip between my thighs. He paused for a moment while I shuddered in his arms, throwing my head back into my pillows and making a complete ass out of myself. When I was finished, I had tears in my eyes, not from an emotional response or anything but just because it felt so damn good.

"Hey beautiful," Quinn whispered after a few seconds.

"It's Andi."

Fuck Valentine's Day

"Do you think you could, um, help me out a little?" Quinn sat back and showed me his, uh, problem. It was about six inches long and totally uncircumcised.

I sort of panicked and shoved him off onto the floor. Not because of the whole not circumcised thing, but because I had just orgasmed in the arms of a guy who hadn't even known my name until like, two days ago.

"Where are you going?" he asked as I stumbled out of bed with the sheets wrapped around my waist. "You've got that condom on your bedside table. You sure you don't want to finish?" I grabbed a bra from the top drawer of my dresser and yanked a random dress off its hanger without bothering to look at what it was.

"Sorry, Quinn. I have to get to calc." I paused. "You should go, too. We have a pop quiz today."

An hour later, I was digging under my seat surreptitiously trying to find my newest clue while Quinn's hand slid up my thigh, once again reminding me that I was wearing a short, black dress and no panties. I am not a commando girl under normal circumstances and I have to say, the extra breeze factor was not all it's cracked up to be.

"You wanna go back to your place after this?" Quinn asked as I slid my eyes over to him and tried not to turn bright as fuck red. His lips were a bit swollen, nicked by my teeth, and he was leaning back, gazing at me from those pretty blue eyes like I was the perfect catch. *Aha!* My hand finally brushed the edge of something, and I grabbed onto it like it was a lifeline.

"Um, not sure," I whispered as Preston Ellis appeared in the corner of my eye, handsome and studious, as always. His glasses were clean and polished, shining under the bright lights as he ascended the steps to the stage and took over for the world's laziest professor, one who thought student assistants were there so he could hit on some of his favorite coeds during class. Namely the ones who sat in the front row and forgot to cross their legs when they wore shirt skirts. Considering my commando status, I didn't just remember, I seriously considered gluing my knees together to keep my bits hidden.

Fuck Valentine's Day

"We're going to be moving on to chapter seven … " Preston began as I dragged my prize out from beneath the seat and set it in my lap. I had to try really, really hard not to keep staring at the cut on his forehead. Or his ass when he turned around. Either way, the man was distracting as all get out.

"I was thinking, if you wanted, we could even go somewhere else, you know. That is, if you're into that kind of thing." I ignored Quinn and examined my clue. It was a wooden box with a red envelope taped to the top. Fortunately, Quinn was too busy checking out my tits to really notice that I had something in my lap much less where it had come from. I opened the envelope first.

You found them. Nice job, Andi. Can I call you Andi? Inside the box you'll find one of my favorite Valentine's Day treats along with your next clue. Enjoy.

I tucked the note into my textbook and cracked open the lid to the box. Inside, layered in pink velvet, were a pair of metal handcuffs. Real nice ones. Fancy ones with a heart shaped key and everything. Goose bumps sprung up all over my skin and I found my pulse racing like I had just run a marathon.

C.M. Stunich

Rational Andi: *Yeah. Seriously. Do you need anymore proof? This fuck is a stalker. Like a big time stalker.*

Horny Andi: *Yum. Handcuffs.*

Rational Andi: *Which this bitch is going to use to attach you to the bumper of his cargo van and drag you along the interstate. Are you insane? Go to the campus police. Now. Get a Doberman pinscher. Something. Anything. Hello? Are you even listening?* Pause. *Aw, go fuck yourself. And don't come crawling to me when you're lit up with seventy-five watts and draped over a brass lamp.*

I slammed the lid shut on the box and cringed when the sound rang out through the quiet space between Preston's words. When I looked up, not only was he staring at me, but so was half the class. *Nice.* I swallowed hard, grabbed Quinn's hand and dragged him out the door. As soon as we hit the pavement, he was pushing me up against a wall and kissing my neck. Whoa. Talk about sending wrong messages. First, I turned him down, then I practically fucked him, and now … wow … I couldn't give a shit less about him. I needed to find

Fuck Valentine's Day

Mystery Man before curiosity really did kill the cat. Or the pussy. Whatever.

"I knew you were hot for me," he whispered as I tried to get my raging hormones under control. Despite what Rational Andi thought, I was intrigued. This guy, whoever he was, had me at *handcuffs*. Damn, but I was falling for him and I hadn't even met him yet.

Rational Andi: *He's probably, like, three hundred friggin' pounds with a hairy beer belly and a lisp.*

I ignored her and pushed Quinn off, using the wooden box to put space between us. He stepped back, but he didn't look happy about it. His hands went straight in his pockets and he puffed out a huge breath of air.

"What's up with you?" he asked me, tilting his head to the side like he was a bird or something. "You are like, a big time faucet." I blinked stupidly back at him.

"Huh?" I asked as the door opened behind me and footsteps approached quickly. I glanced over my shoulder and found Preston coming towards us with a frown on his face.

"You know, the whole 'hot-cold' thing?"

"Excuse me," Preston said as he stepped between us,

totally cutting off Quinn from sight. I looked up, up, up and tried to focus on the small white bandage on his forehead instead of the fire in his eyes. And believe you me, it was burning in those big brown orbs nice and *hot*. "But you dropped these." He reached out a hand and showed me a pair of pink and white striped panties that were totally *not* mine.

Rational Andi: *They're from your fucking stalker, you dumb ass. You dropped them after you made an ass out of yourself. The professor was the one that found them and picked them up, friggin' sniffed them, and tried to bring them out to you. You're lucky Preston was there to interfere.*

I did not ask my rational mind how she knew things that I clearly did not (or maybe she was just guessing) and accepted the panties gratefully. After all, I wasn't wearing any. Maybe I could just slip into the bathroom and put them on?

"Wow, this is awkward," I said as Preston stepped back and revealed the empty space where Quinn had been. *That asshat!* I thought angrily as I looked around and found hide nor hair of him. "But, uh, thanks, and sorry."

Fuck Valentine's Day

Preston's right brow quirked, just the one. "You know for, uh, hurting your head and all."

"My *head* is fine," he said and somehow, I got this sort of flirty vibe from him. It gave me the chills down my spine. "But what I'd really like to know is how you managed to drop your underwear in a lecture hall. Doesn't happen everyday, you know." I paused and opened my mouth to explain, but I was a pretty shitty liar, so nothing came out but air and more spit. Yep, I was a drooler for sure. *Attractive, Andi. Nice job.*

"I have to go," I said as I turned away suddenly. Preston caught my arm at the last second, spun me to face him and pulled me close, kissing the hell out of me as I struggled to grasp two things. First, was that geeky Preston was a better kisser than badass Quinn, and second, that his hand was creeping down my back towards my ass. I shoved him in the chest, not because I wanted to, but because he was dangerously close to discovering that I was commando and tried to come up with something to say. Two years I had stalked Preston and only now was anything happening because of it. Maybe he'd been crushing on me all that time, too? But no, I wasn't that lucky.

"Don't be a stranger," he said, and then he turned around and disappeared back into the auditorium leaving me even more confused than I'd been earlier. Twenty-two years and hardly any interest from the opposite sex. Now, suddenly, just days before the worst holiday of the year, I was getting crushed on by not one but two, possibly three (including my stalker), guys? What the heck?

Rational Andi: *You're exuding whore pheromones. Put on some damn Chanel or some shit. Cover up that crap.*

Horny Andi: *Go to hell and rot.*

I stuffed the panties in my book bag and peeled the envelope off of the handcuff box. I'm not going to lie and say I wasn't *this* close to chasing after Preston Ellis and using my new gift on him, but I did have priorities. First of which was finding my mystery man and determining if I was going to kiss him at first sight or have him arrested. Either of which was fine by me so long as I got my inner monologue down to a few lines a day. At this point, Rational Andi and Horny Andi were just two steps away from putting me into an insane asylum.

Fuck Valentine's Day

Congratulations. You're getting better at this. Tomorrow, after your lit class, there will be a clue attached to the bulletin board outside the classroom door. I'm not going to give you any hints, but you should know which one's mine. Try not to have too much fun with these without me.

I crumbled the note up in frustration and shoved it into my bag along with the handcuff box. So the little bitch was going to drag this out and make me wait. Fine. I could do that. I could handle the wait. The question was, could my libido?

CHAP 4
A RANDOM ACT OF
FELLATIO

FOUR DAYS UNTIL STUFFY, CLINGY,
CODEPENDENT COUPLES' DAY

"So then Preston just – " I slammed the butts of my palms together for emphasis. "Up and kisses me. And by that time, Quinn was nowhere to be seen. He just split without a single word, and then he was waiting for me at my car later; I don't even know how he knew which one was mine. I just walked into the parking lot and BAM, there he was, leaning on the hood like a fucking porn star. Nothing happened after that. I didn't even say *hi* to him because I was kind of pissed off. I mean, seriously, what the fuck?" I paused. I wanted to tell Gen about the handcuffs, but I was afraid she was going to be judgmental. Still, she was my best friend, so I just went for it and opened up. I prefaced my words with, "I really appreciate you being such a good listener."

"Oh, baby," Gen cried out as Lance drove into her and the couch springs went into overload. I was standing in the downstairs bathroom looking into the mirror, wishing the two of them would stop fucking, so I could finish my conversation. In all honesty, I was there first and Gen really, truly was listening, and then that asshat piece of shit had to saunter in and then well, I might as well have turned invisible. They had their pants off before I was even off the couch. I saw Lance's dick for the first time and let me just say, I wasn't very impressed.

"Mystery Man has a much nicer cock," I said to the reflection who was posing as my fictional, best friend Gen, the one I wished Genevieve Pares would be, but never could because she was too self centered and probably a nymphomaniac. "But what I am supposed to think about the handcuffs? Is he spying on me through my window or something, or is it just a coincidence?

Either way, I mean it is creepy, but I just can't get him out of my head. If I was to take all the guys I've ever really had a thing for, it would go like this: Mystery Man, Preston Ellis, Quinn Prentis, and Jake Tandor."

Rational Andi: *Jake Tandor was a douche.*

Regular Andi: *Can you please stop? You and Horny Andi are like days away from putting me into an institution.*

Horny Andi: *That's your own damn fault. Go get laid.*

Rational Andi: *Yeah, seriously, that's your problem. You do need to get laid. I can't deny it anymore. The situation has spiraled out of control. You don't want them to remake the 'Forty Year Old Virgin' eighteen years from now – with you as the main character.*

Horny Andi: *Yeah, and they won't even have to write a script. They'll just do a documentary and it will be twice as funny.*

Rational Andi: *Good one, Horny, that was hilarious. Totally. Totally.*

"Goddamn, I am fucked up," I said as I tried to ignore the very early signs of Schizophrenia and trudged back up to my room to get dressed. I had little butterflies in my stomach, butterflies that were completely and utterly convinced that today was the day where I finally met the man whose cock had been riding around in my bag for days. I was certain that he was going to reveal himself to me in the most romantic way, sweep me off my feet, and show me a good time. He was going to be tall with dark hair and blue eyes, muscular but not beefy, and kind. His lovemaking was going to be so perfect, so on point that the Gods themselves would invite him to join them on Mount Olympus. He was –

Rational Andi: *Dear God, can you please shut the fuck up?*

I sighed, and pulled out of my fantasies. I wasn't an idiot, okay? It wasn't like I didn't realize how stupid I sounded. A guy sent me a picture of his dick in the mail. That's fucking weird. Still, I couldn't help but follow this thing to the end. As long as he didn't ask me to meet him in a dark alley alone and unarmed in the middle of the night, I figured I was okay.

So I dressed myself in a pair of red skinny jeans, a black tank top, some tennis shoes, and a winter coat and headed to class.

Quinn was waiting for me when I arrived.

"Hey there, Andi," he said, and it honestly took me several seconds to respond as he'd never used my actual name before. Impressive. Very impressive. Quinn grinned at me and nibbled at his sexy lip. His Mohawk was in full form, nice and spiky and straight up and down, gelled to perfection. Despite the chill winter air, he was wearing a white tank that did everything to show off his muscular arms and his myriad tattoos, and nothing to ward off the chill of winter.

"Aren't you freezing to death?" I asked him as I shivered and glanced surreptitiously over at the bulletin board. It was absolutely covered in crap. There were ads for roommates, for tutors, for summer jobs; there were sales flyers for the local mall and the campus bookstore, even ads proclaiming their need for a sexual partner to spend Valentine's Day with. How the hell was I supposed to find Price Albert in all of that? Hmm? I was hoping to hell that he was going to be a tad less mysterious this time or I would never be able to find my next clue, and I wanted it. Oh trust me, I *wanted* it.

Fuck Valentine's Day

"I was until you showed up," Quinn said, stepping forward and wrapping his arms around my waist. I was going to protest, to bark at him for disappearing on me yesterday, when his warm lips pressed against mine and silenced all logical thought. *Mmm.*

"Did you miss me as much as I missed you?" Quinn asked as he pulled back and threw a lascivious wink my way. He brushed the hair from my face as I struggled to come up with something to say.

"Um, no," I said which was the honest truth. I hadn't missed him, not really. I'd *thought* about him, but then, that isn't really the same thing, now is it? Besides, I hardly knew the guy. Wet humping aside, we'd barely spoken a dozen words to one another. "Anyway, I didn't appreciate you running off yesterday. Where the hell did you go?" Quinn rubbed at his face with his hand and tried to play off his reaction as nonchalant when I could see that in reality, something was bothering him. The tattoos on his fingers danced enticingly before me as he pretended to itch his face.

"You seemed pretty comfortable with that teacher," he said, no doubt referencing Preston Ellis. "Like maybe you knew him or something?"

I blinked and tried not to sound stupid when I said, "Huh?" The strange tone in Quinn's voice was not jealously (though it would've been nice if it had been), but rather something else. Fear, I think. *What the hell?*

"Why?" I asked as Quinn's head followed the ass of a very hot, very blonde coed into the doors of our lit class. I rolled my eyes and tried to resist the urge to punch him in the stomach. I wished Scar Face was there, if only briefly, so he could do it for me. Bet that would've gotten Quinn's undivided attention. "Let's get to class," I said as I moved away, certain that I didn't want to miss today's lecture on the importance of grammar in dissertations. Much as that subject fascinated me, I had other thoughts on the brain. Still, it wouldn't do to hang outside and wait. If I did then my secret admirer might see me there and decide not to approach. I couldn't let that happen. If this guy escaped without me knowing who he was, I was going to be awfully ticked off. Or maybe I was just really horny. That can cause severe mood swings and changes in behavior, you now.

"Are you sure you want to go class?" Quinn asked as

Fuck Valentine's Day

he leaned in for another kiss and tried to press the aching bulge of his erection against me. I resisted the urge to just let go and let him do what he wanted to do. I wanted it, really, really wanted it, but it would definitely not do for my stalker – I mean secret admirer! – to catch me playing bump and grind with Mr. Tattooed, Sexy and Fuckable. Even if he was an ass. I watched as his gaze caught on the jiggling goodies of yet another coed and slapped his arm.

"Seriously?" I said, and he shrugged, holding out his elbow for me to take as he lead us into the darkness of the lecture hall and found us a pair of seats off from everyone else near the back of the room. There was a slide show up front titled *The Life of the Comma – Her Use, Abuse, and Effect on Modern Literary Writing.* Snore! My eyelids were already creeping down and getting ready for a catnap. This hour was going to stretch into eternity while my mind spun a million different ways that this could all end. Or not. My secret admirer might never want to reveal himself. What if he wanted to play this cat and mouse game forever? Then what would I do? Pick the next guy in line? I shivered and tried not to think too hard about my kiss from Preston Ellis. I didn't know how to address it. Did I seek him out and ask him? I didn't even know where he lived. My best bet was to wait for my calc class next week and see what he had to say to me, if anything.

Don't be a stranger.

What the hell did that mean? Quinn, who thought he was being subtle but wasn't, began to moan from next to me, and it only took me about three seconds to realize what he was doing with his backpack sitting on his lap and his hand buried beneath it. He was jacking off. In the middle of class. Holy cupcake!

"Quinn," I began, but he just winked at me.

"Thought this might help you get in the mood," he said, and I was struck with the urge to both punch him and kiss him at the same time. Immediately, my body alerted me to my situations on the feeling by becoming quite moist and rather excited at the idea of this public display of indecency. I mean, after all, this was not something that I had encountered on a regular basis and the unusual, to me, was rather arousing.

Rational Andi: *Or maybe you're just a desperate virgin?*

Fuck Valentine's Day

I squelched my thoughts and tried to focus on the proper way to use a comma with conjunctions while I tried to ignore the soft murmurs falling from Quinn's round, sexy lips. The man had a porn star mouth, no joke. It was all moist and hot and shaped like a bow tie. I swallowed hard and tightened my fingers around the ends of my armrests.

"Come on, Andi," Quinn whispered, all husky and sexy. "I told you, you don't have to touch me if you don't want to, but you could always touch yourself." I leaned towards him, convinced that the brunette two seats up and three over could hear us and would soon stand up and announce our debauchery for all of the class to hear.

"I am not going to have a mutual masturbation session with you in the middle of a lecture." And then, feeling satisfied that I'd made my point, I leaned back and kept my gaze pointed forward. Quinn continued to, uh, *spank it,* while I continued (and failed) to ignore the noises from down under.

"Did you bring lube?" I whispered as the wet, slick sound from next door increased in volume.

"Yeah," he whispered, eyes hazy and far away. "I

don't like to whack it dry; it decreases sensitivity." I put a hand up to shield my face from his giddy, loopy, droopy one and tried not to sigh.

"Thanks for sharing," I said as I shifted and squeezed my thighs together tightly. This whole situation was just weird and totally *wrong,* but it was also kind of hot. Super hot. Like, tear-off-your-panties-and-straddle-that-bitch hot. *Maybe if I just reached down and sort of stroked myself through my jeans ...* I shook my head to clear it and took a deep, cleansing breath.

"When you're using commas to indicate a natural pause in a sentence, you must be very careful not to – " My gaze wandered back to Quinn who was still going at it like he was at home in his dorm room, oblivious, carefree. I couldn't help but wonder how many girls he'd done this very same thing with. I decided not to ask. It would only make the situation that much worse.

"Join me, beautiful," he said as he stroked his cock with rapid fire movements that made my head spin. "I can't come unless I know you're doing it, too."

"Then I guess you're just going to be stuck in blue ball land because there is no way in hell that I'm touching myself, okay? You're hot and all, but I'm just not comfortable with PDAs." I paused. PDA was not the right word. This was not a public display of affection, this was a public display of absolute, complete, and utter lack of self-control. I mean, I bet the man jacked it a dozen times a day in the privacy of his own home. Did he really need to do it in public, too?

"Oh God," he moaned and this time, I wasn't imagining it. Brunette Girl turned around to look at us and gave Quinn a very confused once over. "I think I'm there, Andi."

"Okay, but can you keep your grunts of pleasure down to a minimum, please?" I whispered, wondering where all of that, you know, *that* stuff was going to go when he actually did finish. I glanced across the aisle at the other empty row and thought about moving away from Quinn when his hand came out of nowhere and cupped me right between the legs.

A moan escaped my lips. A very loud, very guttural, very husky moan that reverberated around the rear rows of the auditorium like it was being played on a surround sound speaker system.

Heads turned, eyes focused, expressions wrinkled.

Shit.

I shoved Quinn's hand away from me and left him with his pants undone and his backpack covering his erection while I hightailed it out of there and stumbled across the cement courtyard to the bulletin board. I grabbed the edge of the wood and dropped my book bag to the ground while I tried to catch my breath.

"Wait up," Quinn called, not as far behind me as I would've liked. "What's the matter? I thought you were interested in me."

"I am," I said as I stayed bent over and tried to breathe. *How many of the students heard? Thirty? Forty? Will they remember my face? Did they know what was happening? Maybe they thought I was having cramps or something? Yeah, that's it. That's my story. I was crampy and didn't have any Midol on me, so I moaned in pain. No big deal, right?*

Rational Andi: *Keep telling yourself that, sugar cakes.*

One day, I was going to commit a random act of violence, and it was going to be against that bitch. If she kept at it, I was going to spend a whole day reading the *Twilight Saga* and see how she liked them apples.

Rational Andi: *No! Please, anything but that! I swear to God, I'll be a good girl.*

I turned to Quinn with a smirk that I don't think he quite understood.

"Cool," he said, and then, "Want to try something fun?"

I stared at him.

"Fun?" I ventured, wanting very much to turn around and examine the bulletin board, but not wanting Quinn to know about my secret admirer. After all, I was saving him in case things didn't work out with Mystery Man or Preston.

"Classes don't end for another forty minutes."

I pursed my lips.

"But that doesn't mean people don't walk by."

"It'll only take a minute."

"What will only take a minute?"

"This." Quinn opened his pants and let his uncircumcised penis hang out like a damn flag, blowing in the wind all graceful and shit.

C.M. Stunich

"Jesus H. Christ, Quinn."

"I'm halfway there," he whispered with his porn star mouth, and then he was all up in my face, kissing my neck and rubbing his erection against me. It was a hard thing to deal with – literally. It was like, rock solid when I reached out and wrapped my fingers around it. *Oooh, velvety. My first, real penis grab. Nice.*

I swallowed hard, and realized that only a complete and utter idiot would go down on their knees and suck a guy in the middle of a courtyard at one of the busiest universities on the West Coast. Idiot then I must be.

I pulled away from Quinn's mouth and sunk down, convinced that I was totally blowing it with my Mystery Man by doing this, but sort of unable to stop myself. I was a kink. Yes, I'll admit that. A virgin kink. Do you know how hard that is? I thought about dirty stuff, dreamed about dirty stuff, and never got to do dirty stuff. Plus, you know, I blamed the upcoming holiday and all of its pushy, lovey crap. Couples everywhere were amping up their PDAs, buying each other kitschy shit, and just generally being assholes to the rest of us that would like to have a sex partner. So maybe it wasn't the 'right' thing to

Fuck Valentine's Day

do, but right and wrong are relative and I *wanted* to do it. I wanted to suck Quinn Prentis's cock.

"Guess the box of chocolates worked?" Quinn joked as I examined my prey and tried to figure out what to do with it. I resisted the urge to flick him in the nuts and tried to concentrate.

"I said I wouldn't touch your dick *just* because you bought me a box of chocolates. This has nothing to do with that." And then I just went for it, wrapped my mouth around the end of Quinn's dick and swirled my tongue around in a circle. His hands came down right away and tangled in my hair for dear life.

"You fucking rock, Andi," Quinn growled which made my heart pump faster and my skin tingle with need. *Shit, this is hot.* I slid my mouth down as far as it would go until I felt the head of Quinn's cock pressing into the back of my throat. "I think I'm in love," he groaned as I slid back, grazing my teeth gently along his skin and pausing as I tried to recall some tips Gen had given me. Whatever she said about sex, I believed because I had the sneaking suspicion that she was a nymphomaniac and she had *plenty* of practice at the art.

C.M. Stunich

Grab the base of his cock with your hand and pump it while you suck the tip. If he's uncircumcised, make sure you move that skin around with your tongue; he'll love that. This doesn't work for all guys, but it's like BJ 101, you know? You can't go wrong with this.

So I did what she said and used my tongue to suck gently on Quinn's foreskin while my hand worked the shaft of his cock. His grip on my hair got tighter and his fingers were almost painful, but there was a pleasure to it that made my lower parts throb and had me wishing I'd taken him up on his offer to go somewhere yesterday. Oh yes, I very much wanted to fuck Mr. Prentis.

"You've got it," he told me and seconds later, he was thrusting into my face and coming. Without really thinking about what I was doing, I swallowed it. It was hot and salty and kind of gross, but also sort of sexy, too. *Goddamn, I'm a pervert.* "Holy shit," Quinn breathed as I stood up and watched him zip his pants in the nick of time. A giggling couple came around the corner of the hedges next to the classroom, swinging their hands and gazing at one another with sheer, unadulterated affection. *Disgusting.* "Please tell me you'll go out with me tonight." I wrinkled my nose and glanced over my shoulder. It only took me about two seconds to find what I was looking for. I spun around right away and just stared.

My secret admirer had left me another Valentine's Day card with yet another hunk o' burning love on the front. I knew it was from him because there was a pink, glittery handcuff sticker on the lower right hand corner. I wondered briefly how he knew I was going to be the first one to get to it when the thought came to me.

"Oh my God, he was watching us," I whispered as Quinn wrapped his arms around my waist and started kissing my neck. My whole body went up in flames and I nearly melted.

"Who was watching us?" he whispered as I reached up and plucked the card from its position next to a green flyer advertising a used motorcycle. "'Cause that's kinda hot."

"Quinn," I said as I spun around and tried not to think about Mystery Man staring at me while I went down on the totally sexy badass/douche bag that was Quinn Prentis. *What was I thinking?* "I'm busy tonight. Call me tomorrow?" And then I took off, forgetting that he didn't even have my number.

CHAP 5
RANDOM SEXUAL ACTS PART TWO OR ANDI FIGURES OUT WHAT SHE WANTS - SORTOF
THREE DAYS UNTIL "YOU OWE ME A BJ BECAUSE I BOUGHT YOU DIAMONDS" DAY

Happy Fucking Valentine's Day, Bitch said the card that my stalker – grr, my secret admirer – left me. Inside, in that tiny, perfect script it also told me that, *I would never talk to you like that – unless you wanted me to. Come find me.* And then there was an address, one that I knew well because it was across the street from the campus.

My Mystery Man lived in Crest Haven Apartments.

I slapped the card against my forehead and tried to breathe. Going to a creepy apartment complex alone was not a good idea. I needed to take someone with me. Gen had already left with Lance for the weekend and I couldn't imagine any of my other friends being much help in a dangerous situation of any sort. They were all limp-wristed toots as far as I was concerned.

I had to call Quinn. Or Preston, I added unconsciously. But then, why would he come along? I mean, he did kiss me, but I still didn't know what that meant. Quinn, well, he owed me. Sort of. I mean, it wasn't like I was a prostitute or anything, but I did blow him off in the courtyard in front of our lit class, so I was guessing that if I asked him out, he'd say yes. I didn't exactly have to tell him what I needed him for, did I?

I stood up, tucked my new card in my handcuff box and picked up my phone to call Quinn. As I scrolled through my contacts, I started to get irritated. It was nearly four in the afternoon and he hadn't called me, not once. Then I got to to the end of the alphabet and realized that he didn't have my number. Fuck.

Now what?

I stood up and kept scrolling, desperate to find someone, anyone, that I thought might be able to protect me against my possibly dangerous secret admirer. I was still of the mind that he was going to be one, hot tamale, but then there was always a chance that my pulsing clit and raging libido were clouding my mind.

Horny Andi: *Why don't you just go hire a hooker? They've got some nice, clean ones in Vegas.*

Rational Andi: *Why fork out the dough when she's got Quinn around? I bet that boy would be damn good in bed. I mean, with the thousands upon thousands of practice sessions he's no doubt participated in, his skill shouldn't even have to be called into question.*

Horny Andi: *He does have tattoos ...*

Rational Andi: *Yes, yes, he does.*

"Would you guys shut the fuck up?" I said aloud which was probably a really bad sign. At least there was nobody around to hear me losing it. That's a good thing, right? I paused in the *P*'s and noticed that I had Preston's number. "When the fuck ... " I began and then remembered that he was once a project leader in my bio class and gave us all his number then. I chewed my lip until it was sore and squeezed my eyes shut. I pressed send and waited with a sick feeling in my gut for Mr. Ellis to answer the phone. It didn't even ring. It was like he was waiting for my call and suddenly, he was just there on the other end of the line.

"I was hoping you'd call," he said and his voice friggin' oozed through the speaker and fucked my ear. *What the hell?*

"Um, hi," I said, and I sounded like a high schooler calling up her crush for the first time. I cleared my throat and tried to sound nonchalant and carefree, like I was just checkin' in about that whole kiss thing or whatever. "Hey, are you familiar with that big white apartment building across the street from the north entrance to campus?"

"Crest Haven?" Preston asked, sounding completely and utterly confused. *Nice, he fucks my ear, and I don't even acknowledge that fact. I've been crushing on this guy for two years, and this is the best I can do?* "Yeah, why?"

"I, um, do you think you might be able to head over there with me today? I have a friend who's sick and needs me to stop by for a second, but I don't trust that neighborhood ... " Preston laughed and my lady parts got all giddy and started sending these tingly signals to my

Fuck Valentine's Day

brain that made me feel like I was floating on candy clouds. *Yummy.*

"Absolutely," Preston said and then paused. "Was that friend me?" he asked and my heart leapt into my throat. *Oh my god ... is it ... is it him?* I swallowed hard, too stunned to speak. If the first and second man on my crush list were one in the same, then Quinn could kiss my ass, because I was going to be handing Preston my virginity with a fucking bow and some sparkly wrapping paper. When I didn't respond, he cleared his throat. "I mean, I live here. I thought you knew that."

Oh.

Rational Andi started to speak, but I silenced her with threats to not only read the *Twilight Saga*, but also to watch it. She went silent.

"Um, no, sorry, but my friend, he lives in ... " I scooted back into my room and checked the card again, just to make sure I had the number right. "Apartment thirty-six." I could practically hear Preston smiling through the phone.

"Ah, that's E.'s apartment. I know him well." I paused.

"E.?"

"Well, that's what all his friends call him over at the boxing gym." Aha. Pieces started to come together. E. I wanted to ask what it stood for, but figured that would kind of blow my cover, so I just laughed and pretended like I'd known that all along.

"Right," I said. "Sorry, I just usually call him by his full name."

"Sure you do," said Preston softly. "Meet you in the lobby in twenty?" I nodded, realized he couldn't hear me and started to speak. Too late I realized he'd already hung up.

Preston was standing outside the glass front doors of the apartment building with a tight, white T-shirt on over some dark blue jeans. His dark hair was slicked back and his glasses were sitting on the bridge of his nose, resting there precariously as he flipped the page in his book and smiled.

I swooned and practically crashed to the sidewalk in a cloud of lust. If Quinn had a porn star mouth, then Preston had a kissable one with soft, full lips that would probably feel good damn good down below as well as up above.

When he looked up and saw me stumbling down the walkway like a drunken idiot, he closed his book and moved forward to greet me, chest muscles bulging gently beneath his shirt. It was just enough of a peek at his body that I not only craved more but absolutely, one hundred percent felt like I had to have it.

"You look really pretty today," he said softly as he hugged his book to his massive chest and smiled gently at me. That whole ear fucking thing seemed a long ways off from the soft spoken man before me, and I couldn't help but wonder what that was all about. *It's always the quiet ones,* my brain thought as I tried to not to mentally measure the width of Preston's biceps.

"Thank you," I told him as we stood several feet apart in awkward silence. "Um, so, apartment thirty-six?" Preston flushed a pink color like he was embarrassed and nodded, turning without a word and leading me to the elevator. The atmosphere was tense and uncomfortable, nothing at all like it had been the moment he kissed me. I wanted to ask about that, but had no clue how to go about broaching the subject, especially when Preston was squished into the corner of the elevator hugging of all things, a copy of *Gone with the Wind*. Definitely a *What the fuck?* moment. Ear fuckers do not read period romance novels. I declined to mention it.

"How long have you known E.?" Preston asked me as the elevator dinged and we stepped into a beige hallway with a horrible burgundy runner and framed oil paintings of fluffy dogs. I shrugged noncommittally.

"Oh, you know," I said vaguely as I waved my hand and tried to pretend like I knew where I was going. Preston paused and pushed his glasses up his nose with two fingers, his middle and his index. Very sexy. Very provocative. I had to swallow my lust down, and it hit me in the gut heavy and hard.

"Apartment thirty-six is the other way," he said, and I blushed.

"Oh, yeah, that's right." I smiled tightly and spun on

my heel. The silence and the anticipation were freaking killing me. *I'm about to meet Mr. Seven Inch. What will I say? What will I do?* "So, how long have *you* known E.?" I asked back and Preston shrugged.

"Oh, you know," he said and we both chuckled at that. *God, I like this man,* I thought as we paused at a white door and my heart skipped a beat, making my whole chest hurt. I was about to meet my Mystery Man, but right now, all I wanted to do was get to know Preston. *Just meet the guy and get it over with. That way, you can get him off your mind and make some decisions.* I sighed and raised my hand to knock.

Bang. Bang. Bang.

I gave Preston a tight-lipped smile and bounced up and down on my heels. Seconds ticked past, long as hours, and nothing happened. I rang the doorbell. Nothing.

"He was expecting you?" Preston asked, and I shrugged, again very vague and nonchalant. "Maybe he's running late?" he added as I continued to stare at the gold numbers on the door with a sinking feeling in my gut. Was Preston scaring him away? Maybe he really was a rapist or a murderer or something? But then, Preston seemed to know him pretty well ... "Want to come over to my place and have a cup of tea or something?" *Aw, tea. Cute. What a nice boy.*

"Sure," I said as I tried to push back my feelings of disappointment. E. would show. He had to. Had to. For my sake and his. I mean, why play this game with me and then just disappear? Anyhow, I knew where he lived now and could do some stalking of my own, maybe tape a pic of my swollen clit to his door and see how he liked that.

Preston turned away, stepped about ten feet and unlocked the very next door. Apartment thirty-seven. Huh.

"Oh, so you're like next door-next door neighbors?" Preston nodded and stepped back, holding out an arm for me to enter. I moved over to his door and stepped inside to the sweet scent of dragon's blood incense and freshly mopped floors that gleamed. *Damn.* Neat and tidy and sexy and toned and wow ... Preston was a one of a kind guy for sure.

"Welcome to my life," he said which I thought was kind of strange until I entered the living room, turned and

Fuck Valentine's Day

saw a … a thing hanging from the doorway to his bedroom. "Darjeeling?" he asked me as I tilted my head to the side and tried to figure out what the black straps attached to the door frame were. "Green? Black? Chai?"

"What is that?" I asked as I pointed at the thing with my finger. Preston stepped up next to me and adjusted his glasses.

"That," he began softly as he set his novel down on the glass coffee table to my right, the one without visible streaks of any kind. "Is a sex swing." And then his voice was all sex again, ear fucking the shit out of me.

I spun quickly and took a step back, certain that Preston was about to go psycho on me. He just stood there and watched me move back.

"I'm in the mood for some green tea if that's okay with you?"

"I think I should leave," I said and then tripped on the edge of his couch, went sprawling back and landed in artfully arranged decorative pillows. Preston moved towards me and put his knee between my legs, leaning in close enough that we could kiss, but somehow maintaining this perfect distance that made my breath catch in my throat and my pulse thunder.

"Why would you want to do that?" he asked me as he lifted his hand and ran his nail down the side of my face. "Then I wouldn't be able to fuck you."

"Um," I said and then all words were knocked right out of my brain by this horribly delicious kiss that Preston gave me, tangling his tongue with mine and drawing me forward without using a single, other part of his body.

I threw my arms around his neck and wrapped my legs around his midsection, completely and utterly forgetting about Quinn and even – get this – Mystery Man. Two years of watching Preston prance his tight ass around campus had gotten to me, and I was not in the mood to hold it back. *Fuck Valentine's Day,* I thought as I once again pushed my lack of self-control onto the holiday's shoulders.

"I … " I tried to speak, but Preston was having none of it, kissing my mouth, my forehead, nibbling my ears and throat, caressing my breasts through my sweater. "We, um … "

"Shut up, Andi," he said as he sat back, grabbed my hips and flipped me over, taking my ass in his hands and

Fuck Valentine's Day

positioning me for … well, for easier access you might say. "The safety word is kitten, but I don't think you'll need it. We'll start slow."

"Kitten?" I asked. "Safety word?"

"Well, it's not likely something you'll say by accident during sex," Preston said as he did something behind me which was, presumably, to free his cock from his pants. "I tend to get rough, so I like to have a safety word, just in case."

"I can't do this," I said suddenly. "I'm a virgin." I tried to stand up, but Preston pushed me down so that my face was buried in fluffy pillows with tassels galore.

"And that means what?" he asked as my skirt came up and my panties came down. "Are you not ready?"

Horny Andi: *Jesus Christ, girl, get it on already. I'm not saying you should give it up to the first prick that comes along, but seriously, it's just your virginity, it's not like you're selling your soul to the devil. Loosen up. You've been stalking Preston for years, remember?*

Rational Andi: *Didn't you write 'Mrs. Fisher-Ellis' on the back of your binder like some grade school twit?*

Regular Andi: *Fuck you both.*

"I'm going to take your silence as an invitation. If you change your mind, you know what to say."

"Kitten?" I asked as my lady bits pulsed and throbbed with need. The sudden exposure to air and Preston's warm bulge pressing against them didn't help me think any clearer. It wasn't until he let go of me and stepped back that I could finally breathe and remember the alphabet.

"I'm sorry," Preston said, and although it was undeniably weird to know he was staring at and talking to my vaginal opening, I didn't stand up. God help me, but I wanted him to plow me hard and fast. There was just one thing that I would not compromise on.

"Condom?" I said, and I swear, I could hear a dirty, sexy grin spread across his handsome face.

"Of course."

As Preston fished out a condom from somewhere on his person and opened the package, I put my hands on the back of the couch and held on for dear life.

Fuck Valentine's Day

"Sweet fucking Jesus!" was the first thing I said when Preston grabbed my hips, cock slick with lube, and thrust all the way into me. He didn't test the waters or ease himself in, he just entered me in one fell swoop and made me wish I had walked right up to him when I'd first seen him and stuck my tongue down his throat.

"Look up," he told me and although I could barely breathe through the intense pleasure radiating out from my pussy and swirling around in my belly, I followed his instruction and found myself face to face with my reflection. Not five feet away was a square mirror propped up on a side table and in it, I could see my hair mussy and disheveled and my eyes cloudy with euphoria and the sweet thrill of sex. Sex. Sex.

"Holy shit," I said – well, drooled. I kind of drooled that.

"Holy shit is right," Preston said as I watched the shimmer of light on the edge of his glasses, the way he tilted his chin up and bit his lip as I pulsed and squeezed around his cock. "You are so fucking tight."

"And you're a wolf in sheep's clothing," I groaned before he screwed the words right out of me and left me absolutely breathless and wanting more, so, so much more. I squeezed my eyes shut, and only opened them because Preston grabbed me by the hair and jerked my head back.

"Watch me fuck you," he told me as he rode me into oblivion. "Watch me take your virginity."

"I don't want to," I whispered as he jerked on my scalp just enough that it was all painful pleasure, hot and stinging, reminding me that my body was a bundle of nerve endings just waiting for the perfect touch.

"Then say what you need to say, Kitty Cat," he told me and I swear, that was what sent me spiraling over the edge, arching my back like, well, like a cat in heat. The super ripped, nerdy guy I'd been crushing on for far too long was pounding me with a cock that rivaled even the *Randy* in thickness and far surpassed it in length. In that moment, Quinn and Mystery Man were so far off my radar that it wasn't even funny.

Fuck Valentine's Day

And that's why I almost murdered Preston when he pulled out of me without warning.

"You bitch!" I screamed as I collapsed into the couch and spun around to glare at Preston's well formed jaw, sculpted cheekbones and sensually curved lips (yes, I was ogling, so sue me). "What the – " I tried to cuss him out, but he took advantage of my open mouth by leaning down and inserting his tongue into the space between *hell* and *fuck you.* I groaned into him, leaning forward and tearing at his white T-shirt like some sort of crazed animal.

"Slow down," Preston said as he pulled back and slid his hands under my ass, lifting me right off the couch with barely a grunt. I slid my arms around his neck and held on for dear life as we moved across the living room as graceful as a pair of dancers. I had to blink several times to stop Rational Andi and Horny Andi from overwhelming me with shouts and cheers of encouragement.

I just lost my friggin' virginity. Shit, well that was easy.

"You're," I began and didn't know how to finish that sentence when Preston slammed my back into the bedroom door with a quirky little snarl playing about this kissable lips. They didn't look so sweet now. More like deadly. Yes, deadly was the word. "Strong."

. "I've been a boxer for almost ten years now," he said and I swear to you, I wet myself in the best of ways at that one word. *Boxer.*

"You're a boxer, too?" I asked, referring to E. who was now disturbingly on my mind again. I wanted to examine Preston's cock, compare it to my dick pic, which was weird, I know. Luckily, I didn't get long to dwell on this eccentricity as my newfound lover was all about getting down to business.

Preston sat me in the black harness and instructed me to grab the two loops that were hanging on either side of my head. He then leaned back and hooked some stirrups around the arches of my feet, all the while stretching each and every movement, every word out, so that it was all a wicked stretch of foreplay.

"Isn't there a learning curve or something?" I whispered breathlessly as Preston teased me with the hard line of his cock, rubbing it across my most sensitive parts as I tried to accustom myself to the fact that I, Andrea Fisher, was sitting in a *sex swing* of all things. "I mean, shouldn't I be tackling basic moves before I move onto the complicated, kinky stuff?"

"Oh?" Preston asked as he slid a few inches into me and made my hands clench around the straps. "You want to stop and lay on the bed while I remove every bit of your clothing with my teeth, nice and slow, agonizing? While I touch your clit with my fingertips, caress your breasts with my mouth, make you scream for it? And only then will I enter you in a nice, easy missionary position. How does that sound?"

"Actually pretty damn good," I said. "But this is better." Preston grinned.

"Good, because it's this first and that later."

And then he thrust into me fully, found my core and manipulated me to within an inch of my life with long, slow strokes. Preston fucked me deep; he fucked me hard, and behind us, the door shook like it was just seconds away from popping off its hinges.

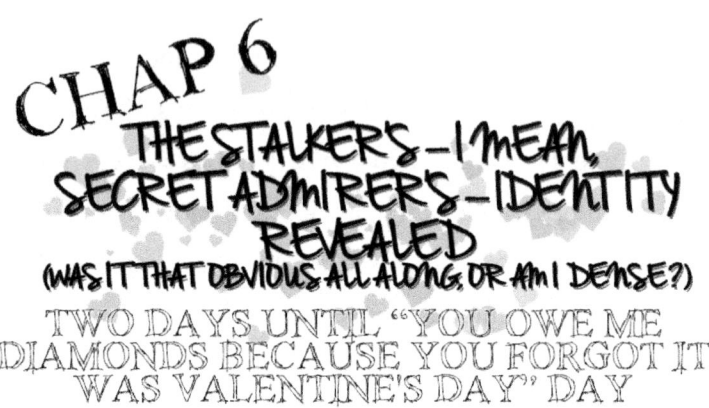

CHAP 6
THE STALKER'S—I MEAN, SECRET ADMIRER'S—IDENTITY REVEALED
(WAS IT THAT OBVIOUS ALL ALONG, OR AM I DENSE?)
TWO DAYS UNTIL "YOU OWE ME DIAMONDS BECAUSE YOU FORGOT IT WAS VALENTINE'S DAY" DAY

I woke up in Preston's bed.

Preston's. Bed.

"Oh shit!" I called out as I sat up and dragged the blankets around my chest like a shield. They were white, perfectly crisp and had the slightest scent of laundry detergent clinging to them with gentle, floral fingers. I bit down on the corner of the comforter and tried to slow the thumping of my heart.

What have I done?

Fuck Valentine's Day

Rational Andi: *Well, you came over here to ask Preston to protect you from the mysterious 'E.' who I still think is planning on turning you into a lampshade and instead, got ravaged by said protector.*

Horny Andi: *It was hot though, you have to admit.*

Rational Andi: *True, it was pretty hot.*

"Shush!" I whispered angrily as I tried to figure out what time it was. The room was dark, but there was some faint light streaming in through the curtains on either side of the bed, highlighting a dresser with absolutely zero clutter on the top, a bookcase stuffed to the gills, and a yellow sticky note taped to the back of the closed door. *The very same door where Preston screwed the shit out of you.* "Preston?" I called tentatively, unsure of 'day after' etiquette. Was this a one night stand or something else?

Rational Andi: *That would've been a good question to ask* before *you let him put his dick in you.*

I stood up, blankets still clutched to my chest. They didn't stay there long. Preston Ellis had perfect hospital corners, the kind that grab onto your linens and refuse to let go. I hadn't seen hospital corners like that since I stayed with my grandma the summer before senior year.

Jesus Christ. I gave up my shield with a huff, and shuffled forward on naked feet.

"Hello?" I asked as I slid across the perfectly polished floor and paused with my face just inches away from the sticky note. Obviously, I was meant to find it since it had my name on it. I blinked the sex hangover out of my eyes and squinted at the tiny, square print.

At the boxing gym. Preston is with me. Come quick. Sincerely, E.

"Holy fuck," I said, wondering what the hell was going on.

Horny Andi: *Yay, a three way!*

I ignored her and ripped the note off the door, found my clothes, and hightailed it the fuck out of there.

I stood outside the gym for a good fifteen minutes, examining the comings and goings of the ripped, tight ass mother fuckers that frequented the old brick building. I even saw Scar Face but decided not to say hi to him when he tossed an evil glare my way.

I shook out my hands and stopped pacing, facing down the burgundy doors with the faded paint for the longest time.

"You can do this, Andi," I said as I raised my chin, puffed out my chest, and marched in there with a single-minded determination. I had to meet this 'E.' and then I would deal with Preston. That is, if there was anything to deal with. Maybe he'd just go back to gently ignoring me? Force me to stare at his ass in calculus without being able to touch? Too cruel.

I was already pissed by the time I entered the dark, sweaty building and found Preston in the ring, covered in sweat, muscles contracting as he dodged his opponent with skillful grace and carefully restrained power. *Yummy.*

"Kick his ass, E.!" one of the dudes on the other side of the ring called out, and although it was very, very difficult to tear my eyes from Preston's nearly perfect form, I did. I let them slide over to his opponent and just froze there.

Aw shit.

Wherever the dick pic had come from, it had not come from this guy who had to be E. (if the shouting dude was any indication). Or if it had, then it had been taken years back when he was in his prime. Many, many years back. He was older, probably in his early fifties, with a hairy back and a pale, almost pasty, belly that while toned, was in no way related to the chiseled beauty that was in my picture. I tried to imagine that gorgeous cock coming out of the old dude's shorts and nearly vomited in my mouth.

Not gonna happen, I thought as Rational Andi guffawed maniacally in the background of my mind. Seriously, this whole hearts and kitty cats Valentine's week was screwing up my game. I was better than this, less desperate than this, surely.

Horny Andi: *At least now you can go after Preston full time.*

I ignored her, too, and watched as the older man put up his arms in surrender. Sweat was pouring down his skin and while Preston looked hot all slicked up and moist, this guy just looked like he needed to shower. I watched as the two men did one of those weird ass half-hug things that guys do where they punch each other in the back and waited for his eyes to fall on me, for his thin lips to smile, for him to approach me and say, *Andi, right? Can I call you Andi?* And then I was going to have to tell him no thank you and hope to God that he didn't try to follow me home and kill me. Nice.

"Good fight, E.," said the pasty man as he lifted off his red, padded helmet and nodded at Preston. As he turned away, his eyes caught on my tits which annoyed the shit out of me, but they didn't linger. In fact, he barely registered me. I gawped at his pube covered back and tried not to look as shocked as I felt. Finally, *finally,* the signals and the clues and the not-so-subtle hints of the past few days were hitting me, and the truth of the matter was very slowly dawning upon my ridiculous person.

"Nice job, E.!" the dude from across the ring called as Preston made his way over to me and leaned down over the ropes. He wasn't wearing his glasses, but he was looking right into and through me like he could see just fine, smiling a nasty smile that promised horribly delicious things, and dripping tiny droplets of sweat onto the cement floor.

"Thanks for coming," he said as I stared back at him, at his hard pecs and sculpted belly, his massive biceps and his mussy hair. *Fuck.*

"You," I said slowly, feeling rather stupid. I mean, the guy had put his damn dick in me and I hadn't bothered to even *look* at the fucking thing. If I had, I would've known much, much sooner. "You're the stalker."

Preston frowned.

"Secret admirer."

"You sent me a picture of your dick."

Preston removed his gloves and hopped over the edge of the ring, landing rather gracefully next to me as he rubbed at his white wrapped wrists.

"I thought you'd like that."

"It was creepy."

Horny Andi: *Liar, liar, pants on fire. You whacked it to that thing more than once.*

"You've been staring at me for years, eye raping me every chance you get."

I gasped and touched a hand to my chest.

"How dare you, you fucking prick," I said as I tried

to control my temper. What he said was true, kind of, so how could I stand here and get all pissy over it?

"I thought you knew it was me all along. Isn't that why you came over to my apartment and played stupid about the whole 'E.' thing?" Preston made quotes with his fingers. When I didn't respond, his eyes got big and round. "Oh my god, you didn't know, you really didn't know." I crossed my arms over my chest and tried to play it cool.

"Did, too."

"Did not."

"Did, too."

"What's E. stand for?" he asked with a smirk as he stepped in closer to me and made my nostrils flare at the warm, heady masculine scent of sweat and sex. *Holy shit.*

"Ellis," I said proudly.

"Lucky guess," Preston said as he slid his warm, wet hand across my jaw and tangled his fingers in my hair.

"No such thing as luck," I said as he pressed his mouth to mine and kissed me with a hot, slick tongue and a gentle scrape of his teeth over my lower lip. "All skill."

"Speaking of skill … "

C.M. Stunich

"Oh God, Preston! *Yes!*" I shouted as my stalker – shit, secret admirer – thrust me into the metal lockers at my back and then proceeded to spin us around and slam me into a tiled wall near the showers. "Don't stop," I growled as I nibbled at the warm skin of his neck and tried not to let out full blown screams in the middle of the locker room. We were alone for now, but I had a feeling that if I let out the kind of bloodcurdling screech that was crouching in the back of my throat, folks would come running.

"Shh," Preston whispered as he somehow managed to maneuver us into the shower stall and close the curtain behind us. *Thank God for coed locker rooms,* I thought as we gained our bit of privacy in the nick of time. Seconds after Preston started slamming me balls to the wall, a group of guys entered the locker room laughing and joking about God only knows what. I sure as hell wasn't listening.

"Oh shit, Preston," I groaned as he thrust into me hot and hard, grinding our hips together at the same time he was reaching around me and switching on the faucet. Warm water cascaded over us and stuck my clothes to my body, plastered my bangs over my eyes and still, I couldn't have cared less. Heat was building up down below, climbing the ladder of my spine up to my brain and exploding in brilliant color behind my eyes. "Fuck me harder!"

"Much as I like the words that are coming out of your dirty, fucking mouth," Preston said, pausing his oh so perfect rhythm long enough that I wanted to stab him in the eye with my nail. "You have to be quiet. We have company."

"Fuck you," I said as I spit out a bit of water at him and watched a smile spread across his mouth, evil and dirty as sin. *Some nerd,* I thought as he pulled away and let my feet drop to the floor. *That whole nice guy thing was a bit of a sham. Preston Ellis is a fucking pervert.*

"If you can't keep quiet, we'll have to move on to a different activity," he said and his voice, for a split second, was sweet as pie, nice and gooey, gentle. Then he was reaching out and grasping me by the shoulders, pushing me down to my knees hard. I hit the tiles with a curse and a small surge of pain. Again, it was just enough to tease my senses, to remind me that I was alive, and not enough to freak me out or damage my body. *Oh my god, I think this shit is getting me off.* I had a sudden and irrational fear that I was going to turn into Anastasia Steele and start spouting off things about my inner goddess and referring to my fucking cunt as *down there.*

"Stop," I said as Preston began to slide his condom off, one painful inch at a time.

"The word is kitten, remember?" he said and then he was tearing the rubber off and flashing me with the dick from my pic. You know when you get a package (pun intended) in the mail and go to review it online and there's always that option that says, *Was this item as described?* Well, Preston's cock was a real life replica of that perfect picture, long and curved and glimmering with a silver ring.

I swallowed hard and closed my eyes. I wanted to suck him off, watch him shudder in my mouth, but I had to put a brief stop to this, just long enough that I could think. I hadn't been doing a whole lot of that since yesterday, so wrapped up was I in this whole secret admirer/Quinn/sex trip I'd been on. There was more to me than just this, sure. I was a kick ass checker player, a fond patron of rare cheeses, and a complete and utter sucker for poorly written romance novels. I had to know that Quinn was after more than just some pet he could parade around on command.

"Kitten," I said and I nearly cried when Preston sighed and squatted down next to me. I reached out and brushed some wet hair from his forehead, desperately wishing that he had on his glasses. Somehow those made him seem easier to talk to.

"What's the matter, Pussy Cat?" he asked and I couldn't help but shiver. "Are we moving too fast?"

"I'm not here to play submissive for you," I said and Preston blinked his big, brown eyes back at me like I was an idiot. It was hard to focus on them when his nipples looked so pert and yummy in the steamy air of the shower. "I don't mind a bit of rough sex," I continued and didn't even blush when I said it. "But I'm not a toy."

C.M. Stunich

Rational Andi: *Told you. You're a fucking perv.*

Horny Andi: *I know, right? Seriously, I wouldn't be surprised if she tried to pash either one of us.*

I told my inner voices to go screw themselves (in the privacy of my own brain, thank you very much) and watched Preston carefully as his smile lost some of its heat and took on some of that studious confidence that had attracted me to him before.

"You know when I first knew that I liked you," he began as he ran his tongue across his moist lips. *Swoon.* "When you gave that presentation in Intro to Genetics." I stared at him for a long moment while the guys outside our shower stall snapped at one another with wet towels and engaged in other questionable behavior.

"I don't get it," I admitted as my body pulsed and begged me to cut the crap and save the heart to hearts for after the big O.

"I could tell you were strong," he continued. "The way you spoke, the conviction in your voice, the confidence in your face. We can play rough, but trust me, I'd never want to break you."

"Is this just about sex?" I ventured. I mean, I wasn't

going to get down on my knees and beg the guy to marry me, but I also knew that I wanted to explore a relationship outside of just the bedroom. I think that's why I'd been so hesitant to hook up with Quinn, despite my intense attraction to the man. I had a feeling that all he really wanted was to bang bodies.

"I hope not," Preston said and that was that, I was done talking. His face was too cute and his mouth, despite being absolutely filthy, really was dangerously kissable. "Andi," he said, pulling back, voice low and husky. "Ever since I watched you go down on Quinn, all I can think about is your mouth." I stared at him, but he didn't let me rest there gawping for long. Instead, Preston rose to his feet in a smooth, graceful motion that had drool threatening to drip from my mouth yet again (thank God for the shower).

"You watched?" I asked, and although I had sort of suspected that all along, it was an odd thing to think about. "You just stood there and watched me suck Quinn's dick?"

"I like to watch," he said and then flashed me his perfect cock for just a moment before grabbing me by the hair and tugging me forward, slipping himself between my lips and burying his dick as far back in my throat as it could go.

"God," he groaned as he began to thrust, and I had to reach out and grasp his shaft before he bruised my throat. I wanted him to press his hips into my face, fuck my mouth like it was a pussy, but I didn't think I could take it all in, so I made do, reaching up and massaging his balls until his breath was ragged and heavy, until he was practically panting for me. "You have no idea how much I've been wanting to do this."

I slid my tongue around the head of Preston's dick, nibbling at his piercing with my teeth as he slid forward with barely restrained passion. I could tell he wanted to pound the shit out of me, but was holding back. *How nice.*

"Tell me I'm better than Quinn," he growled, but I could in no way indulge him with that bit of ego petting. My mouth was full of him, hard and insistent. When I didn't answer, Preston began to get more vigorous, driving into my face with such fury that he was really testing the limits of my gag reflex. Just when I was about to give up and call uncle, or kitten, whatever, he grabbed my hair hard, drew tears from my eyes and shot his wad into the back of my throat. When he pulled back, he knelt down and kissed the fuck out of me, swirling the taste of him around in both our mouths. His cum was sweeter than Quinn's, less salty. *Who knew jizz came in different flavors? Guess you learn something new everyday.*

I put my hands up on Preston's chest and pushed him back as I forced myself to swallow the unfamiliar taste.

"My turn?" I asked, and honestly, I wasn't surprised when he was more than happy to oblige. Pervert is as pervert does, I suppose. Lucky me.

CHAP 7
PRESTON WANTS ME TO WHAT?!
ONE DAY UNTIL EVERYTHING I SAY SOUNDS BITTER DAY

So I sat through calculus with my panties in a tizzy and my heart beating an ode to Preston's ass as he took over for our pervy professor and started working out equations from the homework I most certainly did not do.

"I stopped by your place three times this weekend," Quinn whispered as he leaned over and stared at me from under the fabric of his red beanie. I should've felt guilty about blowing him and then getting with Preston, but I didn't. I was a modern woman along for the ride, and frankly, I was enjoying myself. Things with Preston had become … interesting, so I was going to go with him. *Sorry Quinn. Hey, no hard feelings. I mean, the guy did send me a dick pic. How romantic was that?*

"Sorry," I whispered back at him, trying to focus on the numbers when all I could really think about were the hours that Preston and I spent in bed last night exploring one another. It was like we couldn't get enough of each other's bodies. I shivered. *Exciting.* Quinn wasn't put off by my sudden lack of interest. I took that to mean that I was quite skilled in the blow job department, but you can think what you want.

"Want to hang out after this?" Quinn asked, totally and completely ignorant to the glares that were being thrown our way. When I'd seen him coming for me, I should've relocated to the back row. Quinn was not a front row sort of a guy. After all, it was a bit hard to spank the monkey when you had three hundred other students at your back.

"What you really mean is, do you want to fuck after class?" I whispered as I thought about the wooden box in my room and the naughty handcuffs that Preston and I had yet to break in. I was looking forward to it though. Believe you me, I was practically creaming my panties at the thought of that metal wrapped around my wrists, of Preston's hard cock splitting me open and pumping into me with fast, furious strokes while I ... I shook my head and pinched the bridge of my nose with my fingers. Seriously, Andi? Get a grip on yourself. Admittedly though, much as I accused Genevieve of being a nympho, I was strongly starting to suspect that I might be one, too. I had to admit that, in my humble opinion, the title of Sex Goddess fit me much better than Old Virgin, so I was sort of happy about that.

"Well, yeah," Quinn said as he slumped back in his seat and proceeded to pick at his black nail polish. "That's pretty much exactly what I meant. I'm not exactly that great at being subtle, you know?" I noticed that the professor was glaring at us, too, which kind of ticked me off because moments before, he'd had his eyes glued to the tits of the busty coed next to him. *I really should go file a sexual harassment case against that bitch,* I thought, and then quickly dismissed the idea. Ms. Busty was going to have to take care of herself. I had plans. With Preston Ellis. Yay me!

"What do you want from me, Quinn?" I asked quietly as I turned to face him and leaned in, so I could really get a good look at his baby blues. "Do you just want to screw me for the hell of it? Do you want to be fuck buddies? Or is this your attempt at redeeming yourself and showing the world that bad boys have hearts, too, and that they're more than capable of teaching the poor campus virgin a thing or two about herself?" Quinn blinked back at me and scratched at the tribal tattoo on his right bicep.

"I just wanted to have some fun," he said without shame. I appreciated his honesty, truly, and smiled. Maybe if Preston hadn't thrown me down and fucked the shit out of me, Quinn and I might have … I shook my head. I wasn't pledging my heart and soul to Preston, but he was interesting to me. Interesting enough that I was done with Quinn.

"Sorry," I told him with a pat on the hand. "Not gonna happen."

"Like it totally didn't happen in the courtyard?" he said, and I rolled my eyes. Still, when I thought back on it, it was kind of hot, especially when I imagined Preston with his hand wrapped around his long dick, pumping his fist as I bobbed my head and swallowed a mouthful of another guy's cum. *Hello world, my name is Andrea Fisher and I enjoy recreational snowboarding, hikes through the beautiful forests of the Northwest, and giving blow jobs in public while an adorable geek-turned-dom whacks it in voyeuristic bliss.*

I snorted at my own joke and drew even more angry glares towards the back of my head. Nice. Now I was not only that weirdo moaning girl (yes, I did overhear someone refer to me as such), but now I was also the freak who sits up front and laughs at their own jokes. I was just glad that Preston wasn't looking my way.

"If you don't have anything to do on Valentine's Day, we could, you know get together and – "

"Have a romantic candlelit dinner for two?" I asked sarcastically. How cheese ball. *I fucking hate Valentine's Day.*

"I was gonna say we could try out some of the positions in the new sex guide I bought on Friday." Quinn bent down and started digging in his bag for said object. I reached out a hand and put a stop to that real quick, surprised that I could still get a bit moist at the thought of Quinn Prentis's uncut cock. *Jesus Christ, Andi, reel it in. You've had a popped cherry for like, two days, and already you're scoping out fresh meat.* I swallowed hard and tried to smile at Quinn.

"I'm sorry, but no, thank you. I have plans." He stared back at me like he was confused, and I have to admit, his porn star mouth looked really good in that little 'O' shape he was sporting.

"I thought you were single." I tried to keep my smile plastered on my face, but it was slipping a bit. How on earth did I explain that Preston was my stalker turned lover? It was sort of a weird situation. My eyes slid carefully over to the platform and caught on Preston's strong, muscular back, and the way he moved so slow and careful, without any hint of the power that was resting dark and deadly under that ugly, blue sweater. When I looked back at Quinn, he was frowning.

"I knew it. You're with that boxer guy, E." I stared at him, feeling quite stupid that I was the last person to get the joke. Apparently even Quinn knew that Preston was a boxer and liked to be referred to by the fifth letter in the alphabet. I must've looked like a royal jackass when I went over to his apartment complex spewing crap. "Guess we're not going to be trying out the Seated Scissors," he said, and I could only guess that he was referring to a position in his book.

"I guess not," I replied.

I was dead wrong.

After class, Quinn veered away from me as I approached Preston and ended up hanging on some long legs near the front door. I think they had heads, too, but it was hard to say since their legs were topped with massive tits and scalps of bleach blonde hair.

"Where is he going?" Preston asked me as I approached him tentatively, unsure as to how our new relationship worked on campus. He hadn't said anything about it, so I assumed we were golden, but it didn't hurt to be cautious.

"Quinn?" I asked, completely and utterly confused. I laid my hands on Preston's chest and wished I could rip off his sweater right then and there and start licking my way down his sexy belly. "Why do you care?"

"Because," Preston began as he shifted his brown eyes from Quinn's back to my face. He smiled and nodded at the professor as he moved past and then flipped him off when his back was turned. "Pervert," he whispered, and then, "We have plans with him."

"With Professor Pervert?" Preston laughed and stepped back from me. I let my hands fall to my sides and tried not to be disappointed that he was pulling away.

"With Quinn," he whispered quietly. "You're going to fuck him." My eyes opened wide and refused to blink as I stared at Preston's face and tried not to think thoughts like, *maybe Rational Andi was right? Maybe he is crazy enough to turn me into a lampshade?*

"You want me to fuck another guy?" I said, and the thought sounded even worse aloud than it had inside my head. Preston nodded and pushed his glasses up his nose. I kept my drool in check, but just barely.

"You have to have experiences before you can make decisions," Preston said as his lips curved up and his eyes flickered with just a hint of jealousy, and a whole lot of lust. "If I'm the only man you've ever been with, how will you be able to judge me?"

"I don't need to judge you," I said to him, thinking that this was all some sort of weird insecurity thing that he was going through. I tried to step forward, but Preston stepped back which infuriated the hell out of me. I squeezed my fists at my sides and tried not to get angry with him. "Why are you doing this?" I asked and he grinned, nice and big, teeth flashing bright for just a moment. *Goddamn, I never knew it was possible for a man in a knitted sweater and khaki pants to look so fucking hot.* He couldn't have been any more attractive to me had he been in a biker gang. I paused on that thought and tried to imagine Preston straddling a hunk of gleaming metal. *Okay, well he would be a tad bit hotter if we was a biker, but not by much.*

"I want you to experience another man," he told me as he closed the distance between us and took a massive breath, one that told me he was holding back, that he really did want to touch me, but that he couldn't. "You better take the chance because it could be the only one you get." I stared into his face and tried to keep myself from leaping into his arms and kissing the shit out of him. "Besides," Preston continued as his gaze slid over my shoulder and across the room to Quinn's overly flirtatious back. "I want to watch."

Quinn was more than happy to escort me back to my place. *Wonder if he'd be so eager if he knew that Preston was following, that he was going to be standing outside my door holding his aching cock in one hand and watching us fuck at his behest.* Let's just say that I kept that thought to myself.

"I'm glad you asked me over," Quinn growled, doing his damnedest to get us into a traffic accident by massaging me between the legs while I tried to navigate a tricky intersection. "You're not going to regret it."

C.M. Stunich

"Quinn," I said as my stomach flip-flopped and my heart raced at the speed of light, pumping hormones through my veins like poison, making me loopy with passion. I wanted Preston. I did. I sort of, kind of wanted to date him and try on my first big girl relationship, *but* this whole scenario was straight out of one of my favorite porn movies and Quinn – despite being a complete and utter douche – was out of a wet dream, so if the guy I liked was not only okay with but *endorsed* the whole thing, why not play along? Why not have some fun? After all, Preston was right in a way. He was the only man I'd ever slept with. Did that mean that I had to fuck another guy to know he was good? No, but it did mean that I was a bit limited on my perception. Maybe this wouldn't have worked for everyone, but it was working hard for me. "Shut the fuck up."

"You are so hot when you talk dirty to me," he whispered as he took off his seat belt and leaned over to breathe hot and heavy against my neck. I had no willpower to stop him, convinced that Preston was looking at us both through the rear window, getting hard and angry at the same time.

Fuck Valentine's Day

Then I nearly killed us both when I came within inches of hitting a parked car and decided enough was enough.

"Save it," I barked and surprisingly, Quinn listened. He sat back and smiled, unzipped his pants and fingered his dick through his fly while I put the pedal to the metal and pulled into my driveway at the same moment that Preston parked his car on the opposite side of the street. The plan was that I'd take Quinn upstairs right away and handcuff him to the bed, so that there'd be no chance he'd get up and somehow find Preston in the doorway.

"You want me to bring my sex guide in?" Quinn asked with raised brows and a sly smirk that he no doubt expected would burn a hole through my panties. I rolled my eyes.

"Get out," I said as I climbed out of the vehicle and started up the steps at lightning speed. Quinn was right behind me, sex book in hand, box of condoms in the other. When I gave him a *look,* he just shrugged.

"I figured we'd probably need these sooner rather than later," he said, and I resisted the urge to punch him again. Quinn was hot as hell, but he was also a little bit stupid.

"Who said you were getting laid?" I asked him as I unlocked the door and started straight up the steps to my room. Quinn closed the door behind me and, of course, didn't lock it which was all part of the plan.

"Look at you," he said as he followed after, so close behind that I could practically feel his hot breath on my skin. "You're not even giving me the grand tour, just heading straight up the stairs. Besides, I could see the way you were breathing in the car. You want me bad. You can say what you want to say to make yourself feel better, but you brought me over here with a single purpose in mind." I stopped at the top of the steps and just stared at him as he came even with me. Quinn did not seem at all disturbed about being used for a booty call. Not one, little bit. "And I figured, why not bring extra condoms, just in case?" he said with a wink. "You can never have too many." I rolled my eyes and showed him into my room.

I was so nervous that I was having a hard time thinking clearly. *I should ease him into this. I can't just expect him to roll over and play bitch for me. I have to be*

Fuck Valentine's Day

calm, cool, collected. Subtle.

"Did you want to be on top or should I?" Quinn asked as he removed his shirt in one smooth motion and tossed it onto the floor. *Lordy, Lordy,* I thought as I stared at the swirls of color on his midsection. His tattoos trailed up and over his pecs, traced his pierced belly button, and disappeared, rather enticingly, into his pants. He wasn't as ripped as Preston, but he had a damn fine body, one that wasn't going to be difficult getting into.

I glanced at the door and fought the urge to lean over and peek out the crack to see if Preston was here yet. If he wasn't, he would be soon. It was just a matter of time.

Without answering Quinn, I moved across the room, flicked open the handcuff box and grabbed the metal in steady hands.

"Nice," Quinn growled, reaching out and grabbing me around the waist. "I love a girl who can get her kink on."

"Good," I said as I opened one of the cuffs and hooked it around Quinn's wrist. "Because that's exactly what I'm going to do." And then I was shoving him down and hooking his hand to my headboard. I don't think he expected it at first because his eyes were wide and unblinking as I grabbed his other wrist and locked him in, nice and secure.

"Holy crap," Quinn said as I swung myself up on the bed and straddled him. *How do you like that, Preston Ellis?* I thought as I grabbed Quinn's face in my hands and thrust my tongue between his lips, taking every ounce of dominance and aggression I had inside of myself and throwing it at Mr. Prentis. I thought that Preston could appreciate that.

I sucked Quinn's sexy, lower lip into my mouth, nicked it with my teeth gently and came up for air, pushing my hair over my shoulder to keep it out of my face.

"You're a nasty bitch," Quinn growled as he thrust his hips up and ground his erection into my crotch. I slapped him lightly on the cheek, surprising even myself.

"No, you're a nasty bitch," I told him as I scooted back and unbuttoned his pants. His cock practically burst out at me, desperate to be free as I tugged his underwear down and freed him, holding him in my hand *hard*. My eyes slid unconsciously over to the door and I swear to

Fuck Valentine's Day

you, I could feel Preston's eyes burning hot and heavy into me. How far he was going to let me go, I had no idea. He said he wanted me to go all the way, but could he handle it? Guess it was time to find out.

I squeezed Preston's dick in my hand and leaned down so that I could run my tongue across it, taste the hot, salty, sweaty length of it as I put my drooling talent to good use and moistened him up for what I was going to call the world's best hand job.

I sat back up and started pumping my fist up and down, using my fingers to tease the extra skin around the head of Quinn's cock, massaging it gently up top and then squeezing harder and harder as I worked my way down to less sensitive areas. He groaned and thrashed, moaning noisily and thankfully, not speaking any nonsense. He was a hell of a lot cuter that way.

I paused just long enough to pull my shirt over my head and toss it to the floor, grabbing back onto Quinn before he had the chance to say anything stupid in the interim. I cupped his balls with my other hand and massaged them gently, all the while completely conscious that Preston was there, stroking himself much the way I was stroking Quinn. It was lighting a fire in my lower belly, soaking my panties and driving me into a frenzy. This whole foreplay thing was not going to last long, not today.

Just as I was about to back off of Quinn and go for a condom, his body shuddered, muscles contracting tightly in his belly as his back arched and he came in my hands, shooting hot cum onto my breasts. I sat there quietly for a moment while Quinn panted and grinned a silly grin that made me want to slap him again. I released him and sat back, resisting the urge to wipe off my chest with my sheets.

"You're really fucking good at that, you know?" he purred as he tossed me a sexy wink and I reached over and pulled his beanie off his head. His Mohawk was not in good form. As of that moment, it was just a red, mussy mess, but it was kind of cute, so I threw the hat to the floor and leaned over to to grab the box of condoms. Hopefully Quinn was as big a stud as he said he was because I was not waiting around for him to get hard. It was now or never. "Are you going to unhook me?" he asked and I gave him a look that said, *Are you fucking*

Fuck Valentine's Day

kidding me?

"No," was all I said as I opened the box and pulled out one of the little, square packages. At first I thought the look of horror I saw dawn on Quinn's face was from the loss of control, like he couldn't handle me being in charge, so I rolled my eyes at him and put a hand on my hip. "Look, I'm going to do what I want to do and you're going to like it." I paused, thinking of Preston and decided that I would follow in his lead. "If you don't like it, you can say – "

"Kitten." The voice came harsh and husky from behind me as Preston reached out and grabbed me around the waist, pulled me off of Quinn, and pressed my face down dangerously close to Mr. Prentis's cock.

"Oh my God!" Quinn screamed though I couldn't blame him. I mean, I knew how this probably looked.

"It's okay," I said as I put my arms out and forced myself up, slapping at Preston's hands with my own. I didn't even need to say the safety word; he knew this required at least some explanation. "Preston is here at my behest." I paused. "Or at his own rather. In fact, he was the one that told me I should invite you here." I stared at

C.M. Stunich

Quinn gawping at me and didn't know what else to say.

"Do you have a problem with that?" Preston asked from behind me, and I glanced over my shoulder just in time to see him free his dick from his pants while adjusting his glasses at the same time with the opposite hand. *Perfection.* Quinn didn't answer, just laid there staring at us both like we were insane. "Good." Preston plucked the condom from my hand and proceeded to slip it over his cock, grabbing my hair and pushing my face down to Quinn's lap. "Suck him off, Kitty Cat. I wanted to see you ride him, but I don't think I'm willing to share."

Preston thrust into me unceremoniously, driving himself all the way in until his hips were slapping my ass and the breath was being fucked out of me. I felt lightheaded and dizzy with the intense fullness of Preston's cock and the warm, hot rhythm of his body rubbing against mine, his hands caressing the soft flesh of my hips and his deep, low groans.

"Get me the fuck out of here," Quinn moaned, but he was hard as a rock, and he didn't say the magic word. "Unhook me, come on."

"I said, suck him," Preston commanded as he

grabbed my hair and forced my mouth onto Quinn's dick, sliding my lips down his shaft as he controlled me with strong, sure motions. My head bobbed up and down as Quinn's cock slammed into the back of my throat and Preston's bumped my cervix.

A scream built in my throat, muffled by Quinn's hot, warm body, as the two men groaned and shuddered around me, firm muscles sliding beneath their skin, breath heavy and husky.

Rational Andi: *Heaven.*

I came hard and fast, clenching around Preston's shaft and holding him there while I spasmed and bit lightly down around Quinn's cock. He came immediately, squirting his load into the back of my throat as I dug my fingers into the hard muscles of his lower belly. My body was so tight that I managed to bring Preston along with me, milking the pleasure out of him and wishing I could feel him unloading himself inside of me. *Note to self, get birth control pills ASAP.*

"Fucking God, Andi," Preston moaned as his fingers bruised my hips and held me still for that final, glorious fucking moment that left the three of us sweaty and

C.M. Stunich

panting and well, admittedly, in a very awkward position.

When I sat up, sliding Quinn from my throat and wiping at my lips with the back of my hand, he was staring at us both like we were either the most interesting or most disturbing people he had ever met in his life. At first, there was this moment there where I really, truly thought he was going to freak as Preston unhooked the handcuffs and freed our possibly unwilling prisoner from the headboard.

Quinn sat up and scratched his tight, ab muscles for a moment before he spoke.

"So," he began. "What are you guys up to next Saturday?"

CHAP 8

I FUCKING HATE CANDY HEARTS

JUDGMENT DAY
AKA VALENTINE'S DAY

"What nasty, dirty, pervy things are we going to do today?" I asked Preston as I stretched out on his bed and tried not to think about the fact that I had just spent three nights in a row at his place. Was that a good sign? A bad one? Guess I would just have to find out the hard way. After all, no matter how hard folks try, no matter how many people claim to have the answers, no matter how many how-to books they publish, dating and love will always remain these big, fat questions marks ready to fuck

C.M. Stunich

you the first chance they get. I was just going to have to learn, live, and love the best I knew how and hope to heck it all worked out for the best.

Preston felt around the nightstand for a moment and slid his glasses onto his face before turning to look at me. Just staring at the black frames was getting me all hot and bothered. I hadn't known this about myself before, but apparently, I had an eyewear fetish. Who knew? Thankfully, he'd told me he only wore his contacts to the gym. The gym. I drooled a bit and had to wipe my face. I was forever going to have very fond memories of that old brick building and the perfectly perfect bit of tonguing I got on the tiled floor of the shower.

"Are we going to use the handcuffs again?" I asked, glancing up at the headboard where the metal rings still hung enticingly. Next time we used them, I was going to tie Preston up and ride him into oblivion. He shook his head and leaned over so that his hot breath was pulsing against my ear.

"Actually, I have something even better planned for you." I shivered and tried not to let his ear fuck completely disable my senses. After all, I wanted to be

Fuck Valentine's Day

ready for whatever dirty things we might be doing next. "Hopefully, it's something you'll never forget," he said, and just as I was relaxing into the pillows, getting ready for him to take me on yet another kinky adventure, Preston was pulling away and sliding off of the bed. "Get dressed, Kitty Cat," he said with a wink. "We've got somewhere special to go."

Okay, so you know how you can hate something so much that you can't see straight? How you can despise it so desperately that it makes you see black, makes your fists curl and your body pulse with adrenaline? Well, that's how I used to feel about Valentine's Day. Maybe it was just because I was horny …

Rational Andi: *It was. You were desperate.*

Or maybe it was just because I was looking for someone to share a special connection with …

Horny Andi: *Nope, it was definitely just about sex.*

C.M. Stunich

But whatever the reason, I despised it with every bit of soul until I walked into apartment thirty-six which was, according to Preston, currently unoccupied, and found the world's cheesiest Valentine's Day setup. And then, despite the corniness and the ridiculous expense Preston must have endured to set it up, I suddenly found myself a goopy, sappy mess.

"Happy Fucking Valentine's Day," Preston whispered from behind me, polished from head to toe and dressed in the world's slickest suit. I stared at the table and the roses and the champagne and stood frozen until my stalker – er, boyfriend? Nah, stalker is less scary than boyfriend – turned on some soft music and swept me into his arms, twirled me across the empty hardwood floor and dipped me low, pausing briefly to press a kiss to my ample cleavage. "I hope it's not too cheesy," he told me as he raised me back up and spun me slowly to a soft rock ballad.

"It's so cheesy, it's practically Gouda," I said and laughed when Preston's brows rose nearly to his hairline. "But I love it. Truly, I do. How long have you been planning this?" He smiled at me and paused us in our

Fuck Valentine's Day

dance so he could tug me against him, press our warm bodies together and look down at me with the slightest sparkle of affection in his eyes. It was just a glimmer, but it was there, and that was all I needed to see. After all, we'd spent the last two years crushing on one another from afar, it was bound to happen at some point.

"Since I sent you the card," he told me as he brought my fingertips to his lips. "I hope you like it."

"Oh," I said as I kissed his mouth, his chin, his neck. "I do." I paused as I glanced over my shoulder at the romantic setup that awaited us. "But honestly, I was sort of hoping you'd spend the day fucking the shit out of me."

"Ah," Preston said as he slid his hands down my back and cupped my ass. "You're a lucky Kitty Cat then because I plan to spend the rest of the day doing just that."

The End

Hell Inc.

Hell Inc.

...Dating is hell. Then again, so
are yetis, fairies and socio-
paths...

C.M. STUNICH

"It wasn't necessarily that I wasn't a fan of fairies. Really. It wasn't that. It was that I wasn't a fan of being taken hostage by a group of fairies."

Ginger's life was already full of clichés – sexy demons in business suits, smart mouthed genies, and angry, French kissing yetis to name a few – so what was wrong with one more? Why shouldn't she have sold her soul to the Devil for three wishes? Brendan Fraser did it in *Bedazzled*, so it couldn't be all bad, right?

Too bad her sexy demon caseworker, Levie, wouldn't put down his romance novels long enough to tell her how to make them. With a slip of the tongue (seriously, all she had to do was say 'I wish?'), Ginger's boring life is now up … well, you know, a certain creek without a paddle.

So whether he likes it not, Levie's going to help Ginger take care of some little problems. Her ex-addict mother is attempting to kidnap her, and on top of it all, Ginger's managed to bestow her 'gift' of supernatural sight on some fellow museum goers. Neither of these would be problems if Hell, Inc.'s genies hadn't mysteriously disappeared. They're the only ones who can undo Ginger's wishes and get her off the hook. If only she could figure out where the hell to find them.

Chapter 1

It's never easy to deal with supernatural creatures, especially when they've got the IQ of a doormat. And the clerk behind the counter wasn't your typical teenage drop out. Nope. This one was a special one. He glared at me with his one eye (which just happened to be lazy and seemed to be staring at the ridiculously bright fluorescent lights above my head instead of at my drowsy face) while I questioned him as to the whereabouts of a very specific item. I was looking for black candles. Spooky, huh? But that's what the newspaper ad had specified and so, that's what I was going to get.

"Um," the clerk, who I suspected was probably a Cyclops, mumbled under his garlic scented breath. It was so bad that I actually had to take a step away from him, press my spine against a display of cheap romance novels, and choke back a sob. His breath was so terrible, in fact, that I thought I saw a puff of green float out past his thin lips and join the CFC gasses in destroying the ozone layer. "I think we've got some Glade Flameless Candles in the clearance aisle. They're eggplant purple, but they look black." I tried not to scowl. The Cyclops didn't know what I needed them for. I thanked him politely and wandered off. Served me right for trying to go to Target for dark arts supplies.

I found the aisle my halitosis challenged friend had been talking about and stared at the little white boxes with their red clearance stickers. *Yeah*, I thought sourly, feeling defeated before I'd even begun. *That's what the Devil wants, candles without flames. In eggplant. Fantastic.* I scooped several of the boxes into my basket anyway and tried to ignore the pixies that were swooping and giggling and pulling my mussy hair. If I swatted at them, if I paid them the tiniest bit of attention, then they would do worse. Had done worse. Focus, attention, *belief*, it was what made them real. When a girl and her mother sauntered into the aisle, tossing their identical peroxide manes and glaring at my ripped jeans and my faded *Shrek* T-shirt, they walked right through them.

The pixies giggled and darted towards their shopping basket, shedding sticky glitter dust all over the white linoleum as they heaved a packet of pens out, twiggy arms straining with the effort, and dropped them on the floor. The mother picked them up absently, hardly noticing what she was doing. I sighed. How nice it would be to live so ignorantly. To not know that anything other than humans walked this world. I squinted my gaze at the shelf and tried not to kick something. It wasn't fair. It just wasn't fair.

But this was why I was doing this. Following the directions in this stupid ad. I picked at my pants pocket until I found the crumbled square of newsprint. As I reread it, I couldn't help but have terrible flashbacks to Brendan Fraser and *Bedazzled.* But he'd been stupid. He hadn't been clear with his wishes. I would be. I'd rattle 'em off like the best of bureaucrats. The key was to be *specific.* Very, very specific. I mouthed the words aloud as I walked, swinging my basket and trying to stay positive.

"WANTED: Souls. Single adults only. We are a professional organization looking for talented persons of marriageable age to enter into a trade agreement. Willing to offer three wishes in exchange for a signed contract. Please contact us at our office by arranging three black candles into a semi-circle in front of a mirror. Anoint with blood. Recite address. Hell Incorporated, 666 Gladiola Lane. This solicitation posted by the Devil. No sales inquiries. Offer ends 08/16."

Okay, so it sounded shady and well, just plain bizarre, but I was getting desperate. Two years out of high school had left me with a crappy apartment and a crappier job. I had no friends (except for Erin, but I didn't even really like her), my family was too busy to ever come and see me (and I never went to see them either, I know, I know), and I had absolutely no romantic prospects of which to speak. Well, there was this guy that worked at our local museum, William T. Smidden's Palace of History, that was pretty smoking hot, but I knew I didn't stand a chance. He always had this group of people swarming around like he was the queen bee, buzzing and nodding and kissing his ass. He was young with sandy hair and a strong jaw and pale eyes that shimmered like the aquamarine jewel on my pinky finger. I raised my hand to my lips and gave the ring a light kiss, pretending for just a moment that it was that man's mouth, confident and strong.

I was so entranced in my thoughts that I forgot about the pixie dust and ended up slipping, rather comically, my legs flying out from under me, worn rubber soles of my shoes parallel with the ceiling for just a moment before I ended up slamming into the floor so hard that I was seeing stars. I knew it was bad because the stars weren't just spots of light; they were yellow and smiling and singing the theme song to *My Little Pony.*

The Cyclops I had spoken with earlier raced towards me, red vest flapping, as he pounded over to me and knelt quickly, waving a hand in front of my face and asking a bunch of stupid questions that I wouldn't have known the answer to even if I hadn't just given myself a concussion.

I waved him away but ended up with the store manager and several rubber necking customers surrounding me, jabbering away, and making my head spin while the pixies laughed and sprinkled more of their sparkling crap over my face and arms. I'd be visible from space for the next week. I groaned and sat up while the manager sweated and mumbled things about lawsuits. I rubbed my head and pointed at my basket, just wanting to get the heck out of there.

"I won't sue you," I said, pointing at the candles and trying not to drool. "But can I have these for free?" The manager licked his lips and nodded. *This is too easy,* my brain tried to convince me. *Ask for more.* "And do you happen to have any chicken blood?"

✳ ✳ ✳

A half an hour later, I was strolling out the automatic doors of the Super Target and mouthing the lyrics to some pop song that I only actually knew half the words to. They hadn't had any chicken blood, but they had given me several containers of chicken hearts. There seemed to be quite a bit of bloody residue sloshing about in the bottom of the Styrofoam containers, so I decided that would count. It would have to. It was getting late, and today was the sixteenth, the last day for me to try the spell.

I trudged up the rickety, cement steps to my apartment and tried to ignore the permanent smell of moth balls and dog urine that seemed to permeate the dreary hallway. My neighbor, Gene, a lady of questionable age with a sneer as sharp as cheddar and a smell to match, kicked open her door and proceeded to glare at me as I fumbled around with my keys. She always did that. Opened her door and stared at me. I think on some deep level that she recognized that there was something different about me. Sometimes people did. Though they never seemed to be able to get what that was. If only I felt confident enough in my own sanity to share the simple fact that I could see things that they didn't. I sighed and managed to get into the eight hundred square foot shit hole before Gene began shouting. She did that, too, sometimes. But that was only because she was crazy. She shouted at everyone: the super, the PG&E guy, the mail lady. That act wasn't just reserved for me.

I slammed the door behind me, locked it, handle, dead bolt, chain, always in that order, and headed immediately for my bedroom. If I was going to meet the Devil, I was going to do it in style.

I found a slinky, skin tight dress as red as a hooker's lipstick, and since I'd bought it used at Goodwill, probably something that had actually been worn by a hooker, and paired that with some black pumps and a quick slash of eyeliner. I grinned at myself in the wavy mirror that hung crookedly on the back of my bedroom door. I was as hot as a book cover bimbo. Perfect. I fluffed my black bob, punctuated by neon streaks of pumpkin-bright orange, courtesy of Punky Colour, and sashayed into the bathroom. I was in a better mood than the day I'd bought my Rabbit Habit, though not by much.

The candles, once I'd taken them out of eight, stiff, plastic layers of protection and about a dozen twist ties, looked absolutely ridiculous arranged around the edge of the porcelain sink in my bathroom. They flickered weakly, the cheap lights inside dimming and brightening in a pathetic imitation of a true candle. I frowned at them as I opened the plastic top to the chicken hearts. They smelled gamey and a little bit like iron, leaving a heavy, metallic burn in the back of my throat.

"God," I choked as I dipped two fingers into the cold, watery bird blood. My spine bucked involuntarily as I rubbed the runny ooze down the side of one candle, and then the next, and the next. Let's just say it didn't get any easier or any less disgusting.

After I was finished, I tossed the unused hearts into the bathroom garbage can and scraped anything resembling so much as a fingerprint off of my skin in an attempt at cleansing myself. Once I had decided that liquid soap, a squirt of shampoo, and half a travel sized bottle of Purell would just about do it, I was ready to begin.

I flicked the lights off and grabbed the newspaper scrap off its temporary home on the back of the toilet. I squinted at the words which were incredibly difficult to read in the flickering light and took a deep breath.

"Hell Incorporated," I began, trying to pitch my voice low so that it came out as eery and mysterious as possible. "666 Gladiola Lane." I set the newspaper down on the edge of the sink next to one of the plastic eggplant monstrosities and waited. And waited. And waited.

Nothing happened.

"Goddamn it," I screeched at myself, fighting back tears and gripping the sides of the mirror with a frenzied fervor. "Why do I do this to myself?"

I had a tendency to get really, *really* involved in things that most people could tell weren't going to work out for the best. It was one of my special talents. I punched the mirror once, in a juvenile fight of rage, cracking the glass and cutting my hand open along with it. Tiny droplets of red dripped into the sink and swirled down the drain, turning the residual water a pinkish color and staining the edges of the white porcelain.

"Ah, hell," I cursed, unaware of the swirling black vortex beneath my feet. "I'm going to need stitches."

And then I was falling down a hole, screaming like a B-list actress in a horror movie, until I found myself landing face first onto some terribly itchy, navy carpeting. I pushed myself up quickly, tugging down my dress in the back in an attempt to cover my ass, before taking a look around.

My exploration ended before it even got started because the very first thing I saw was the demon.

And he was pissed.

*Available online at Amazon.com, Barnes & Noble, and Kobo

Broken Pasts

Broken Pasts

C.M. STUNICH

"Until Nathaniel Sutherland was open and all his soul was bared for me to see, I wouldn't be satisfied."

Theresa McMaster does not have a good track record when it comes to men. Her first husband walked out on her after a terrible miscarriage left her unable to carry any children of her own, and her estranged second husband has revealed himself to be more than just an emotional danger – he's been stalking her.

Fearing for her own safety as well as that of her family, Theresa hires a private security service and meets Nathaniel, the man whose secrets and heartaches may just outnumber her own. Drawn into the arms of the sexy stranger, Theresa fears that both of their pasts may very well be the things that keep them apart.

*C*hapter One

"I swear to God, if you don't leave me alone, I'm going to file a restraining order against you," I screamed in the middle of the grocery store. Faces turned to look at me, most of them lined with the telltale signs of age. Wrinkled mouths pursed angrily and older men in polo shirts snorted gruffly. I adjusted my stained tank top and tried to hide my flannel pajama pants behind my cart. "Stop calling me, Gary," I said, lowering my voice to a whisper. Yelling wasn't helping; it had yet to get him off my case before. All I was doing was pissing off the other early morning shoppers. Normally I wouldn't have come out at this time, but I needed alcohol. Hard alcohol. I was thinking Jägermeister.

"But I love you," he told me as I rolled my eyes and tried to keep to the edge of the cereal aisle. When we'd first broken up, all I'd wanted was for Gary to call. Now I couldn't get him to stop. "I want to be with you, Theresa. I'm sorry." He paused and I could hear him breathing against the receiver. "Look, I didn't mean what I said, please. Let's just get back together." I shook my head, not caring that he wasn't there to see me. If I never saw Gary's face again, that would be more than enough for me. The things he'd said, the things he'd threatened, I would never forget those. I had given him a second chance and that had been one too many.

"I'm hanging up now, Gary. Don't call me again." I ended the call and threw the phone in my purse. It promptly started ringing again. I pulled it back out, turned it to silent and put it away. *Thirty missed calls in two days. Incredible.* I wrote it off as simple desperation. I knew what it was like to be lonely. It wasn't easy, especially not for someone as emotionally shallow as Gary Harper.

I grabbed a couple boxes of cereal without looking at them and tossed them into the cart. *Purple, red, pink.* As long as they were colorful, Rhea would eat them. I smiled. Rhea was like the wick that kept me burning. Without her, I would've gone out a long time ago. *But you still need oil,* I thought as I turned the corner and forced myself to go down the next aisle. I was not checking out at eight in the morning with a few boxes of cereal and a bottle of Jäger. If I was going to keep my dignity in check, I was going to at least pretend I was just here to buy the week's groceries. Somehow I made it into the ice cream aisle without realizing it, and stood staring at the pints of chocolate. If I was going to spend New Year's Eve by myself, I might as well enjoy it. I opened the glass door to the freezer and pulled out several cartons, refusing to look at the calorie count on the back. It wasn't like it mattered anyway. I was thirty-two, single, and hopelessly alone.

With a sigh, I continued my shopping and was halfway across the parking lot, grocery bags in hand when I saw him. Gary was leaning against my car with his arms crossed over his chest. I paused near the cart return and debated turning around and heading back into the store when he saw me. He raced over and rescued one of the drooping bags from my tired arms.

"God, Theresa," he said with a chuckle. "What have you got in there?" I walked quickly ahead of him and unlocked the trunk. I tossed my bag in first and whirled to face him.

"You can't keep doing this," I said as I stared him down. He was still handsome, of course, but in a shallow way. I knew what kind of person lurked behind those warm, brown eyes, the rush of anger that had clenched that perfect, square jaw. I'd been afraid he was going to hit me, really afraid. That was something I was never going to go through again. I had the gun to prove it. It was stashed in a drawer at home, brand new and unused. I was going to learn how to use it someday soon, but I hadn't yet gotten around to it. Seeing him in the parking lot made me wish I'd already done that. "This is getting weird, Gary. How did you even know I was here?" He put the grocery bag in the trunk and stepped back, hands up like he was trying to prove his own innocence.

"I didn't know you were here," he said with a shrug. "I just stopped in to pick up some things and saw your car, that's all. Come on, Theresa, what do you take for me?" He tried to reach out and touch me, but I pulled away.

"That's enough, Gary," I said as I moved around to the driver's side of the Camry. "Just sign the divorce papers and let's be done with this." I didn't wait for him to answer, just climbed into the vehicle and started the car. With barely a glance in his direction, I pulled out of the space and left the parking lot. Five minutes later, when I checked my phone, I already had two missed calls. "What the hell is wrong with you?" I wondered as I saw that the most recent was from Gary. With a sigh, I skipped past it and returned the other call.

"Theresa, don't say a word," Jamie said as a chorus of 'Mom!'s echoed in the background. "I've only got a minute. All of Joel's family is here for the barbeque."

"I'm not intruding on your family time, Jamie," I protested before she could ask again. She shushed me and shouted something about cupcakes to the assorted children that were no doubt driving her completely nuts.

"That's not what I'm calling for. It's like beating a dead horse trying to get you to come over here." I heard quite a few *ewws* in response to her idiom. "Is Rhea with Glen tonight?" I wrinkled my face as I pulled into my driveway and turned off the car.

"Rhea is spending the week in Hawaii with Glen," I said as I tried not to sound disappointed. Glen had three other daughters; I only had one. The least he could've done was let her spend the holiday with me. Sometimes, I had the feeling that Glen would be happy if something were to happen to me. I wasn't Rhea's biological mother after all. If I gave him the chance, he'd slap his new wife's name on the adoption papers before the ink was even dry on my death certificate. It was not a good feeling. I had one crazy ex-husband and one vindictive one.

"Great," Jamie said as I climbed out of the car and opened the trunk. "Then you're free tonight?" I grunted noncommittally, unsure where this was going. "Then let me set you up. Joel's friend, Stuart, is in town and he's – " I groaned.

"Stop playing romantic comedy cliché roulette with my life," I said as I tucked the phone against my shoulder and grabbed a bag in each hand. My big hips came in handy, working in unison with my elbows to create a shelf for the groceries as I struggled to shut the trunk. "You set me up with Gary and look where that went."

"Yeah," Jamie said as she put something in her mouth and

tried to talk around it. "It led to a marriage."

"It lasted six months," I said as I set the bags down on my front porch and tried to reason with Jamie. It wasn't easy: she was a prosecutor for a living. "And now he's calling me a hundred times a day and 'bumping'," I made little quotes with my fingers even though there was no one there to see. My neighbors probably thought I was crazy. "Into me at the grocery store."

"So he's stalking you?" she asked, but she didn't sound concerned. It was the first time I had thought of Gary in that way. It would not be the last. "All the more reason to go out with Stuart tonight."

"I already have a date with a pint of ice cream and a glass of Jäger."

"Now who's romantic comedy cliché?" she asked, pulling whatever it was she'd put in her mouth, out. It was probably a lollipop. Jamie had some oral fixation issues that were a frequented topic on girls' night and, according to her, the reason she had such a peaceful marriage. *Long as he returns the favor,* she'd always say.

"I'm not romantic comedy cliché," I said as I finally got the door unlocked. "More like tearful drama cliché." Jamie sighed and I could just visualize her, dark hair pulled back, eyes narrowed and rolling. "Besides, think about what you're saying. *Stuart.* Stuart. Think about calling that out in bed. I just can't imagine screaming Stuart in the throes of passion." I slid the bags of groceries into the house and went inside, locking the door behind me.

"Then call him Stu," she said as I heard Joel shouting behind her about Kool-Aid on the carpet. "Just say yes or I'm going to have to call him back and tell him not to pick you up at your place tonight at six." I groaned and slid down the wood of the door, already fishing around in the grocery bag for my Jäger. I was going to need it to get through another blind date. I twisted the top off, took a swig and sighed my deep, heavy, *I give up* sigh. "Perfect," Jamie said as she kissed the receiver and put the lollipop back in her mouth. "Tall, dark, and handsome will see you at your door, dressed to kill." She paused. "Goddamn it, boys, don't put cold meat on the grill." I smiled as Jamie returned her attention back to me. "I gotta go. Men these days don't even know how to barbeque right. What's wrong with society today?" She ended the call on that note as I stood up and tried to convince myself that I was going to have a good night.

"I should've just gone to the damned barbeque," I said to no one as I picked up the groceries and tried to figure out what the hell I was going to wear.

*Available online at Amazon.com

Tasting Never

Tasting Never

Never say Never

C.M. STUNICH

"Never Ross wants to be loved. It's that simple, but it's not that easy."

Never is a girl with a broken soul who doesn't date nice guys and can't seem to go to bed at night without crying herself to sleep. She doesn't need any complications in her life, especially not when they're attached to a man that could be her emotional twin.

Ty McCabe can't stand Never the first time he meets her. He's aware that the feeling's mutual and the two don't think they'll ever see each other again, but when fate takes a hand and puts them both in the wrong place at the wrong time, Ty and Never form a tentative friendship that opens the door on their dark sides and shows them what it's like to live in the light.

"Sometimes, the only way to go forward, is to take a few, careful steps back."

1

Rick is a perfectly nice guy.

But not for me.

Rick is the kind of guy you can take home to your family, show off, and know that at the end of the day, he'll be there for you. I'm not into guys like Rick. I should be, but I'm not. I think there's something wrong with me. I need a guy like Rick to put me on the straight and narrow, to help me stop doing the things I shouldn't be doing and start doing the things I should.

Right now, my back is to a wall and I'm kissing the neck of a guy I don't know. My therapist says it's because I have 'daddy' issues. Like that's supposed to mean something to me. How can I have daddy issues when I barely knew the prick? He didn't walk out on me and mom like my therapist thinks. She thinks that because I've never told her the truth. My dad died right in front of my eyes, called out my name seconds before the light went out of his face and left him cold. That's all I remember about him. Other than that, my mind is a blank, a series of shadowy pictures without words. They don't make any fucking sense.

The guy I'm kissing unbuttons his pants. I think about telling him to use a condom, but I just don't feel like it. I'm on the pill anyway. He thrusts into me while I'm watching Rick through a crack in the door. He's drinking punch, not alcohol, and smiling with big, wide teeth in a face that's handsome, but not too handsome. Rick's the kind of guy that your friends compliment you on, tell you he's gorgeous, but they never try to sleep with him. The ones they really want, the dangerous ones, the ones with pasts that burn like fire and melt everything around them ... Those are the guys that I always seem to fall for. The one I'm having sex with right now is one of those. I don't even know his name.

"I love you," the guy says over and over, and I roll my eyes. I've heard it before, a hundred times, and I just don't want to hear it anymore. I pretend to have an orgasm, moaning and groaning and scratching his back, and all the while, I'm watching Rick. We have a date tomorrow night that I think I'm going to cancel. I thought maybe I'd take Rick out, see how chivalrous he really was, but tonight, he's wearing khaki pants and a red sweater. I don't date guys like Rick.

The guy I'm fucking finishes and tells me how great I am.

Then he disappears and I don't see him again, not that night or any other. I light a cigarette and leave the room before any of the drunken idiots at the party stumble in and find me there with my panties around my ankles. I step out of them and stuff them in my pocket, aware that my skirt is too short and that my ass is hanging out. I just can't seem to find it in myself to care.

"Hey," Rick says, intercepting me before I can reach the front door. "We still on for tomorrow night?" He looks me up and down, and I can see that he's curious about my disheveled appearance, my mussy hair and my swollen lips, but he doesn't ask about it. I don't think he even gives it a second thought. Rick doesn't know that girls like me exist. He's heard about them on TV, maybe even masturbates to them, but he doesn't really believe that they exist in this world or any other. I really should keep my date with Rick, go out with him, and grow up.

"I can't," I say, biting my lip seductively and touching his cashmere sweater with a shaking hand. I don't know why it's shaking, but I don't like it, so I pull it back and let it fall to my side. I blow cigarette smoke in Rick's face which is rude, but that I do anyway. There's a monster inside of me, eating little bits of me everyday, and I can't seem to stop it. It makes me do things I don't want to do, say things I don't want to say. It makes me tell Rick that I've got to study for a test that he really believes I have.

I kiss him on the lips and leave an orange-red stain before I walk out the door and down the front steps. People wave at me as I go by and say they'll see me around, but I don't really know who any of them are, so I avoid their stares and their friendly smiles. It's all fake, just a big load of shit that I can't buy into or I'll die. If I ever believe in something again, and it turns out to be false, then not only will my body crumble beneath me, but so will my soul. I'll disintegrate, disappear into the wind and blow away. I'll be nothing. I'll blank out and the energy of who I was will just go away, melt into the ground and come back as something unimportant, like a dandelion or a caterpillar. I can't find it in my heart to care.

I walk back to the dorms because I don't have a car. My roommate isn't home which doesn't surprise me. She's in love with another girl, one that's straight as an arrow. They have sleepovers in her dorm room and 'practice' kissing one another like they're in high school or something. That's fine with me because it means I have the room all to myself, gives me a chance to be alone. I feel most comfortable that way. When you're alone, there's nobody there to hurt you or let you down. It feels too good to have that guarantee of solitude.

I fall on my back on the bed and try to breathe through the tears that come to me unbidden. I don't want them, never asked for them. I couldn't even tell you what I was crying over or why. I just do. Every night, I lay here and I try to find something in myself to live for. Every night, I fail and wonder if I need a guy like Rick to show me the way. But then, I'm a big girl, and a feminist, too, so why do I think a guy could save my soul?

I never thought to wonder if I was looking at it the wrong way, if maybe it wasn't a guy that I was looking for, just a person. And maybe I didn't need them to save my soul, just to give me the other half of it. Maybe that was it?

2

The next morning I wake up and have to force myself out of bed. It's a weekend which makes things so much worse. On days when I have class, I have a purpose, an obligation that I have to fulfill. On weekends, I just wait around for something to happen. Today, my roommate comes home early looking happier than usual. I wonder if she scored with the other chick, but I hope not. If so, then she's setting herself up for failure because that girl, whose name I don't know, is the type that grows up and looks for a guy like Rick. They get married and have babies and think they're happy because that's what people like Rick and this other girl do. They think they're happy because they don't know any better. I do. Not because I know what it's like to be happy, but because I know what it's like to be miserable. If you live your whole life in the darkness, then you don't have any trouble recognizing the light.

"There's a party at one of the frat houses tonight, do you want to go?"

"Which one?" I ask. Lacey, my roommate, doesn't know because she doesn't give a shit about frat houses. She doesn't give a shit about men at all. I wish I was like her. Maybe if I was into girls, I'd have an easier time falling in love with someone that wasn't a complete piece of shit? But then again, Rick isn't a complete piece of shit, and I don't want to fall in love with him either.

Lacey shrugs and takes off her sweater, tossing it over her computer chair.

"It's tonight at six, do you want to go?"

"Any party that starts at six is a party that I'm not interested in," I tell her as I stand up and stretch. Lacey gives me a weird look, and I notice that my skirt's ridden up a bit. I push it down and gather up some clothes. I feel disgusting. I didn't change last night, and I can feel that guy's sweat all over me.

"Come with me, please," Lacey begs, and I know she's afraid to go alone because her girlfriend might ignore her and run off with some frat boy. It's happened before. "I'll give you twenty bucks."

"Keep your money," I tell her as I grab a towel and the basket that holds my shampoo. "I'll go, okay? I'll meet you here tonight."

"Five thirty," Lacey says to me with a smile as she brushes a comb through her pretty, blonde hair. "I don't want to be late." I try not to roll my eyes and tell her that nobody gives a fuck if you're late to a frat party.

"Sure," I say as I leave the room in a hurry, rushing to get to the bathroom before everyone else does. There's this communal atmosphere that descends over the room when there's more than three girls in the bathroom at one time. I don't understand it, and it makes me uncomfortable. I never join in the conversation and have to use the stall at the very end, the one with the broken faucet, so I don't have to look at them looking at me and wondering what the hell is wrong.

I get to the bathroom just in time and manage to shower, get dressed, and put on makeup before anybody else comes in. When they do, they're all wearing blue and yellow face paint and talking about *the game.* I don't know if it's football or basketball or baseball, but what I do know is that it's an integral part of their lives that I don't understand. I leave as quickly as I can and head back to my room, toss my stuff on the floor next to my bed, and stand there for a very, very long time.

When I spy the book on the desk next to my bed, I feel a sense of relief. Reading. I can get lost in a world and spend days there. Besides, reading a book gives me a goal. It's that sense of purpose that puts a temporary bandage over my uncertainty and lets me waste away the rest of the day without anymore negative thoughts.

About the Author

C.M. Stunich was raised under a cover of fog in the area known simply as Eureka, CA. A mysterious place, this strange, arboreal land nursed Caitlin's (yes, that's her name!) desire to write strange fiction novels about wicked monsters, magical trains, and Nemean Lions (Google it!). She currently enjoys drag queens, having too many cats, and tribal bellydance.

She can be reached at author@cmstunich.com, and loves to hear from her readers. Ms. Stunich also wrote this biography and has no idea why she decided to refer to herself in the third person.

Happy reading and carpe diem!

www.cmstunich.com

Printed in Great Britain
by Amazon